THE MAN WITH FIFTY COMPLAINTS

Each page had to be perfect; there could be no appearance of erasures, x'ings out, of fumbling uncertainty and mind-changing. A back-aching, eye-straining job, and not on the big sumptuous electric he was used to at work, but an old manual. Fresh ribbon, though, crisp white bond paper. If he said so himself, it looked impressive. Authoritative.

Hc made his covering letter brief and brisk. Mustn't sound peevish, complaining, long-winded. Mustn't come over as some kind of crank. Just an introduction to the hard facts which were to follow . . .

Books you will enjoy from Keyhole Crime:

POSTHUMOUS PAPERS by Robert Barnard
THE LIME PIT by Jonathan Valin
DOUBLE BLUFF by Dell Shannon
IN COLD PURSUIT by Ursula Curtiss
AN AMATEUR CORPSE by Simon Brett
THE IMPOSTOR by Helen McCloy
THE RIDGWAY WOMEN by Richard Neely
RALLY TO KILL by Bill Knox
DEATH SET TO MUSIC by Mark Hebden
STAR LIGHT, STAR BRIGHT by Stanley Ellin
THE DREAM WALKER by Charlotte Armstrong
BEJEWELLED DEATH by Marian Babson
THE DEADEST THING YOU EVER SAW by Jonathan Ross
EVERY SECOND THURSDAY by Emma Page
ONE DIP DEAD by Aaron Marc Stein

THE MAN WITH FIFTY COMPLAINTS

Mary McMullen

KEYHOLE CRIME
London · Sydney

First published in Great Britain 1980 by
Robert Hale Limited

This edition published 1982 by
Keyhole Crime, 15–16 Brook's Mews,
London W1A 1DR

ISBN 0 263 73980 5

The characters and situations in this book are entirely imaginary and bear no relation to any real person or actual happening.

06/0882

Made and printed in Great Britain by
Cox & Wyman Ltd, Reading

To Verna

THE MAN WITH FIFTY COMPLAINTS

Go to the top. "Marcus Bela, Chairman, Bela, Inc., Bela Court, Geneva, Switzerland. Confidential."

No street address needed, Bela was one of those thunderous multinational names, like Shell, or I. T. T.

"Dear Mr., Monsieur, Herr? Bela:

"In the interests of a company of which I have been an employee"—Lester Timmons crossed out "employee" and replaced it with "member"—"for twenty-five years, I feel it a duty to call to your attention a number of deplorable practices, to be documented with facts and figures, that I have noted in the new Bela installation in Goodwood, New Jersey."

It needed polishing and expanding, but leave that until he'd finished composing his list. Planning his introduction, though, was cheering.

"What number are you up to, Les?" asked Oliver, passing his desk. "In your complaint list, I mean."

If it had been any other man, Timmons would have left the question unanswered, but he liked and trusted Oliver Lee. Oliver rated that rarest word of his: Oliver was okay. The grave hazel eyes were mildly amused, but that was okay too; Oliver seemed to find amusement in a great many things that merely angered or annoyed other people.

"Seventeen," he said. "But I only started, when was it?—May twenty-seventh."

It had been, for Timmons, a bitter day in May.

Not as far as nature went. The new young dogwood on the little front lawn blazed white in the sun, and a robin was singing in it when for the first time in his life he slapped his wife's face.

It was a Tuesday.

On Monday, Oliver had asked him to lunch. "Leave your brown bag with your salami sandwich or whatever's in it, probably an orange too, and let's go lean on a nice bosomy bar and have a drink and a steak. Monday has to be dealt with one way or another."

Oliver usually went off and ate alone, and Timmons was flattered.

They drove in Timmons' car to the Ginger Inn and found places at the far end of the bar, where it turned a corner. Timmons was glad the angle partly hid them from most of the tables and booths. If there were other people there from Bela, they might think it was funny that he was having a drink in the middle of the day. A boozer, they'd call him.

Oliver ordered a martini and Timmons a manhattan. Sipping it carefully, he was saying, "I hope it doesn't go to my head," when he saw his wife come in with a very big, heavy-shouldered man. Thick dark hair, big cheeky rosy face already needing a shave by noon. Hand on his wife's arm, hand that knew her, hand that didn't want to stay away from her even in a public place, guiding her into a booth. When she sat down, her back was to him.

He made a little choking noise.

"Drink gone down the wrong throat?" Oliver asked.

"No . . . it's strong, though." Thank God Oliver had never met his wife. He wouldn't recognize her; head bent to the man's head, they were touching glasses now, she was having a whiskey sour and he had a highball in his hand.

"That's what drink is all about," Oliver said. The pretty barmaid leaned on her elbows in front of him and said, "To save you the trouble, medium rare, your honor, sliced tomatoes and hold the dressing?"

"Yes thanks. Same for you, Les?"

Timmons couldn't keep his eyes off the booth. What if she turned around looking for the waitress and saw him? For some reason he couldn't bear to have Oliver know, guess—guess *what?* He certainly hadn't known, and he lived with her for twenty years. The wives of the Oliver Lees of the world—he was a widower but even so—did not meet other men in dark bars for lunch. Especially without telling their husbands about it.

He managed to down the rest of his drink and they both noticed that his hand was shaking.

"I feel a little—" He looked desperately to his left and saw that there was another door, an exit to the parking lot that made an ell around the restaurant. "My stomach suddenly . . . I don't know what . . ."

Run, flee, before an encounter was forced, between him and Lara and Lara's . . . whatever he was. "I'll wait for you in the car, Oliver, I need air, don't hurry with your lunch."

Oliver gave him a kindly puzzled look and thought that perhaps subjecting Timmons to a manhattan at lunchtime was tantamount to seducing a Girl Scout. He had only asked him in the first place because he was vaguely sorry for him.

In a way, Timmons reminded him of one of his brothers-in-law, Rosalie's favorite, Denis. In a handsome gifted family, a loser, in the cruel American terminology. After having failed at his fifth job, four of them obtained for him by his powerful corporation-law father, and subsequently been rejected by a girl he loved, he apologetically put his head in his gas oven. In this final project he was successful.

During the afternoon, Timmons' hand often approached his telephone and was as often withdrawn. This wasn't the kind of thing you discussed over the telephone.

And someone might hear his side of it. He sat in an open pool, in the Department of Merchandising, Packaging, and Sales Promotion, desks to the left of him, desks in front and behind him. To his right was Oliver's modest cubicle. "Plywood from the belt down, glass from the belt up, so you can be seen to be engaged in honest toil," Oliver said. But at least enclosed, Timmons thought, partly private, a label on a man, a flower in his buttonhole.

He tried to concentrate on an account of a softball game for the *Bela Beacon.* Getting out the bi-monthly company news bulletin was one of his major responsibilities. When he wasn't busy on that, there were the booklets, dressily known as brochures, for medical mailings; a lot of fine print, a lot of work.

Brent, the personnel manager, had once referred to Timmons with a smile as "our odds-and-ends man," and in time this had been, inevitably, repeated to him.

In a way it was a relief, a breathing space, that he wasn't able to go home at the end of the day's work, but must cover the bowling tournament between Accounting and Billing, and Research and Development. People were slack and getting more so every day. They should cover their own activities, but they didn't, and the four single-spaced pages of the bulletin had to be filled top to bottom.

It was Lara's club night. She had left him a cold dinner, sliced boiled ham, potato salad from a store carton, and a crisp tasteless wedge of iceberg lettuce with thick orange bottled dressing puddling around it. Timmons had once allowed himself to tell himself, as a cook she's not only careless and lazy, she's terrible.

Reading the newspaper, watching television, he rehearsed. He'd stand and, quietly and strongly, crumple the newspaper in his fist. "Lara. *Who was that man?*"

It got to be eleven o'clock and then 11:30. Maybe she wasn't at the club at all, maybe she was out with that man? But if he called the club to find out, sooner or later some woman would tell her about it . . . "Your husband wanted to know if you were here at all tonight . . ."

It wouldn't do to have a scene at this hour; he wouldn't sleep. He thought fleetingly how nice, how comfortable it would be to look the other way, not bring the matter up at all. If you denied things their existence, they didn't for you exist. But—

He took an indigestion tablet, as the mayonnaise on the potato salad had tasted stale and greasy, and the bottled dressing wasn't sitting well either. He locked up the house but left the front door unbolted. Dangerous. The house across the street, identical to his, had been robbed last month, TV set, stereo, two cameras, but what could he do about it?

He brushed his teeth and got into his pajamas and went to bed, where plain fatigue won over worry and tension and sent him down into sleep.

The robin sang.

"That damned bird, why can't he shut up!" Lara said. "I've got this headache."

She was named after the lead in her mother's favorite daytime serial, "One Woman's World." She was under Timmons' height, about five-six, but she had more bulk and substance than he. Her face was pale and square, her eyes dark, darting, inspecting. She dyed her thick hair, now up in lavender rollers, a bright aggressive brown. Physically strong, she was accustomed to leaning on her mate, sometimes quite heavily. At forty-three, she retained much of her young-woman vitality, most of it turned inward to keep herself enjoying what she could wrest out of life.

Timmons had reached the age of fifty (he had no idea how much he would mind that) in April, and she had said, "Happy birthday." And then, "No two ways about it, I s'pose a person's first half century is the better part of their life. By far. Oh well. I'll buy a nice cake."

If Oliver had a wife, Timmons thought, she wouldn't turn up at breakfast in curlers. If you could call this breakfast, she leaning against the counter eating a piece of toast, he with his corn flakes at the table by the window.

Do it. *Do* it. He had no newspaper to crumple. His heart was pounding.

"Lara. Who was that man you were with yesterday at the Ginger Inn?"

She gave him one long slow blink that surprised him by

reminding him of the descending eyelids of a pet alligator he had had as a small boy.

"Were you there too? Is that what I pack your lunch for?"

He got up from the table, not liking the feeling of her looming over him, crunching her toast.

He hated the tremble in his voice. "Lara, I insist . . . I *demand* . . ."

"For God's sake, just an old friend I haven't seen since before we were married, he's a salesman, boiler fittings, and was passing through town and he said he thought, why not look up good old Lara? Good, yes, I told him. Old, no."

"You haven't seen him for *twenty* years? From the way he was touching you . . ."

"*Touching* me! Are you accusing me of misbehaving before a whole roomful of people?" Red blotched her pale cheeks. "If you think for one minute you're going to supervise my life, Lester Timmons, say where and when I can come and go and what friends I eat with, yesterday or any other day, forget it."

His hand seemed to decide on the action without orders from his brain. The sound of the slap echoed in the kitchen, drowning the robin's song.

He saw, close-up, the incredulous flare in the dark eyes. Now she'll use those words of hers, that truck-driver language, he thought. Or maybe not. I don't now what she'll do, I never hit her before.

She backed away a couple of steps and drew in a long breath. She smiled. "Go to work, little man, mustn't be late. Be sure to be home on time. I'll have a nice surprise waiting for you."

TWO

What would the nice surprise be? That she'd temporarily left him, gone to her mother's? Probably.

He was not, repeat not, going to call her and apologize.

He was sure she had been lying to him, about the old friend from twenty years back.

Or almost sure.

He completed a description of the after-hours engagement party of Clarisse Kelly in Bela Building 11A. The rough version had been written by Miss Kelly, who appeared to be—at least on her own projects—quite unequipped in the matters of spelling and grammar for her work as a typist.

—Still, when you did bump into an old, old friend, unexpectedly begin remembering things together, laughing at the memories together—

At 11:10, he called home to apologize. There was no answer. Out, or just not wanting to give him the satisfaction of picking up the phone and listening to the stumbling words.

He'd try her again after lunch. If he didn't get her before five, when his workday was over, maybe bring home chocolates, or roses. Like someone out of a comic strip, Timmons told himself. No, there was a better, bolder idea. Something he should have done a month, two months ago, instead of just sitting, waiting, hoping that the next time he opened his salary envelope there'd be—

Brent, the personnel manager, was too busy to see him, he was informed, but Mr. Kalish, his assistant, could give him ten minutes at 3:15.

He felt a thirsty need for yesterday's strong drink, but he

sat at his desk, hearing and not hearing the voices, the telephones, the scurry around him. There were eighteen desks and six drawing boards in the pool. He ate the lunch she had prepared before the slap, processed American cheese sandwich with a thin smear of mustard, hard sour tangerine, three chocolate chip cookies.

Look here, Mr. Kalish—

He wanted coffee from the machine, but he thought it might make him even more nervous. It would be nice if Oliver was in his cubicle, Oliver's presence in some strange way reassured and strengthened him. Oliver didn't take any crap from anyone, he thought, or maybe it was that Oliver was invulnerable to crap.

The interview with Mr. Kalish was short. Timmons thought he heard Brent's voice and vocabulary in the younger man's mouth; and his technique in sitting silent while Timmons spoke his piece.

"Good afternoon. You're a busy man and so am I. I'll come straight to the point." His voice was too high; pull it down. "I understand, or, say it's common knowledge, that cost-of-living raises have been given pretty generally because of the move here, new houses to be bought and so on, and prices going up the way they are, food, utilities, doctors, dentists, everything . . ."

Silence. Kalish studied Timmons' tie and Timmons wondered if there was a spot or stain on it and touched it with a hand that shook a little.

"The thing is—I mean, when can I expect mine? I frankly thought I'd have it well before now."

"Ah," Kalish said. "You don't seem to see what a good point you've made. Everything's going up for Bela too. Soaring. Sky-rocketing. Everything from raw materials to the toilet paper in the lavatories." His buzzer sounded and he said into the intercom, "Three minutes, Joan," and then to Timmons, "It's no kindness to hold out vague hopes, is it. I'll be frank too. No, nothing in the forseeable future. In fact"—he picked up a little plastic ruler and seemed to be measuring the length of his forefinger with it—"you might look at it this way: You're lucky you made it here at all. As you know there are a great many people who one way or another were dispensed with in the move."

You're lucky we kept you instead of firing you, Timmons. The hell with your twenty-five years.

Words heard echoing in a greenish smothering tunnel . . . "nothing in the forseeable future."

Nothing. Nothing. Nothing, Timmons.

It's not that I'm lucky, it's that every company I guess needs an odds-and-ends man. A contented, obedient, nothing man.

He got up from his chair. "Well, then, thanks," hating himself for the three words but not knowing how otherwise to make a decent exit.

Tell her, or don't tell her? Keep the scald to himself? But she'd been at him for weeks. "Don't let them think they can trample all over you. I know for a fact that Coggins—his wife told me—went from twenty thousand to twenty-two, the week after he got here."

He worried badly during the drive home, through the terrible Jersey litter of used-car lots, graveyards, gas stations, fast-food restaurants, battalions of signboards, neoned bars, shopping malls that had never heard of trees or grass but only knew the spawn of automobiles, impermanent-looking developments with names like Emerald Hill or Buttercup Ridge.

His own new house, frighteningly mortgaged, was in a development called Golden Valley. "Sounds like a place for the elderly, or senior citizens, or something," Lara had said when he told her about it. She hadn't wanted to be bothered shopping around for houses in the March cold and rain.

"Well, you said new, and washer and drier, and wall-to-wall, and enclosed garage, and we can only afford so much, so . . ."

In April she looked at the three houses to which he had patiently narrowed down the choice and, grumbling, settled for the one in Golden Valley. "The kitchen's half as big as what I'm used to, and the patio is about the size of a doghouse, but at least it's fenced, you can't see those screaming brats but you can sure hear them."

Timmons put his car in the garage and went through the inside door into the kitchen, still wretchedly undecided about telling her or not.

A nausea of hate suddenly rose in his throat, for Kalish, for Bela, for the people, the world, that had brought him to this moment in this kitchen, divested of himself.

Nothing in the forseeable future. Nowhere to turn and no place to go.

Take your punishment at work and now get it at home, right between the eyes?

It turned out that he didn't have to go into the matter, with Lara, immediately.

The man from the Ginger Inn, the big heavy-shouldered man with the cheeky rosy dark-jawed face, was lolling, legs outstretched, at the end of the sofa and Lara was sitting beside him, her face flushed and her hair tumbled. On the coffee table in front of them were two beaded bottles of cold beer and two froth-marked glasses.

"We have company, Les," his wife said. "Meet Frank Rainer. We were discussing him at breakfast, remember?"

Rainer heaved himself to his feet. He looked half abashed and half amused. He held out his hand. He was six inches taller than Timmons. His hand couldn't not be shaken. Timmons shook it.

He took an unkind mental photograph of himself as he performed this social act. Thin, but not in any way trim about the waist and buttocks, where the sit-all-day accumulation was. Slightly stooped, a burden somewhere at the back of his neck and upper shoulders. Faded brown hair, side-parted. Blue eyes with a tired pink on the edges of the underlids. Bifocals rimmed in thin gold metal— "For God's sake, bifocals, but at least you can get young-looking rims," Lara had said.

Gray suit, old but in cared-for condition; white shirt with a thin conservative blue stripe in it; dark red tie, fake-embroidered with a heraldic device.

Up this close, he saw that Rainer's eyes were blue too, a ridiculous baby-blue under fiercely black heavy eyebrows. He was aware of Lara watching the two of them, looking not only pink and tousled but cream-fed.

"Frank has this appointment in Farms River tomorrow," she said. "He'd given up his motel room when the client called. So I said, hell, come on over and spend the night."

Rainer sat down again and in doing so knocked over his half-full bottle of beer. Foam splashed on the sofa.

"Watch it," Lara said, laughing. "Les won't want to sleep in a pool of beer tonight."

"You always were a great kidder, Lara," Rainer said, laughing beerily himself. "Do I smell those steaks? Three minutes each side, I told you."

Bewildered, and not knowing how he should feel about this visit and this visitor until he had time to think about it, Timmons sat down to one of the best meals his wife had served in years. T-bone steaks. Frozen succotash and baked sweet potatoes. Tomato and onion salad with a Roquefort dressing. Hot buttermilk rolls.

"I'll pour the wine," Rainer said.

"Wine on top of beer?" Timmons inquired politely of Lara.

"Why not? Tonight's special."

"None for me, thanks," Timmons said, beginning to know how he should be feeling. Angry.

Rainer and Lara talked about people whose names he didn't know, and laughed, and ate and drank heartily. For dessert, there was vanilla ice cream with chocolate sauce and pecans, and fresh hot coffee, stronger than Timmons was used to at home.

"Frank likes his coffee strong," Lara said, watching his face. "Another cup, Frank?" Waiting on him, solicitous, as she never waited on her husband.

What had she meant, about his not wanting to sleep on a beer-dampened sofa?

There was no guest room in the house.

"I'll have a nice surprise waiting for you."

Rainer resumed his place on the sofa and sighed with contentment. "Little highball'd go good. Or not so little."

"I'll get us one," Lara said. "Les has to work tomorrow, he'd better not. His stomach bothers him. Gas and heartburn and things."

"I don't know what the hell's wrong with me that I never have anything wrong with me," Rainer said.

Timmons sat in a hard cretonne-covered slipper chair facing the sofa and the coffee table. Should I read my newspaper? Or try to join in the conversation as if this was just an ordinary visit? What should I *do*?

Go up to bed, leave them to their mirth and their Four Roses? But *they* could use the sofa—

This is my wife. This is my house. Act like it.

He made himself yawn, and looked at his watch. "If you don't mind, I think I'll go on up, Lara, it's getting late. I'm sure your guest will excuse me." His tone came near suggesting that her guest excuse his way through the front door.

"Didn't you get the message, Les?" Lara asked. "Didn't you hear me say, *spend* the night? And we're not ready for bed yet. Not by a long shot."

Throw the man out. But he's too big and he's part-way drunk. Maybe a broken jaw or worse.

Call the police. What, show his shame? "Officer, my wife has a friend here, a man, she's going to sleep with him in my own bed."

A stranger, a man he didn't know, said from a distance, "Well, it's of no consequence to me." The stranger got up out of the slipper chair, went into the kitchen, took his raincoat off the hook by the door, went into the garage, and got into the seven-year-old Ford two-door sedan.

A little alarmed, Rainer asked, "Where's he going? What's he going to do?"

"Nowhere, and nothing," Lara said. "He can't go to bed and he can't stand the sight of us, so the car's the only place."

"Jeez, you're pushing the guy pretty hard, Lally." A private name coined for her when they had met, three months before.

"He asked for it," Lara said. "Anyway, about going someplace, we'd hear the garage doors opening. Listen . . . absolutely nothing."

For ten minutes or so, Timmons considered turning on the engine and closing the windows. Painless, they said, you just drifted off, and over, and down.

It was Kalish who stopped him. That smug bastard, he thought, sitting there condescending to me. "Not in the forseeable future . . ." He'd heard things about Kalish. Rumors. He was married, but it was whispered that he liked boys, the younger the better.

Now, what could be done with that?

He got into the back of the car and stretched out on the seat with his raincoat wrapping him. His mind flickered and jerked and, gathering speed, raced and roared.

Not just Kalish. All the bloody lot of them. The men and women who had leaped over him and gone up and up, the young who were being so lavishly rewarded because they were young.

Revenge poured through his veins like brandy. No, not just revenge, Timmons said, and then wondered if he'd spoken out loud. Justice. Truth shall out. People thinking they can get away with things forever.

But they can't. Not with me around.

Between uneasy bouts of nightmared sleep, he mentally began his list.

By seven in the morning, he was up to number six.

"Oh, look, Les, we didn't *do* anything. We just sat up and had a few more drinks and played poker, I took ten dollars off him, and about two-thirty, three, he left. It was just to show you not to slap me around, ever again."

Lara was disturbed and curious about him, his tight calm, his pink cheeks and overly bright eyes. He had gone upstairs, found her in bed alone, passed through the bedroom without speaking to her, and taken his usual long hot shower.

She got up during his shower, put on her robe, and went down and as a change from his corn flakes scrambled two eggs for him and made cinnamon-raisin toast.

Eating his rubbery eggs, Timmons said austerely, "I don't think any good purpose will be served by talking about it, Lara. What's done is done."

She didn't like the sound of that. *Done?* He was her husband, her roof, her food, her clothes, her way of life. He made what she thought of as a sort-of-decent salary, and then there was his pension, and the lavish group life insurance policy Bela carried for him, paying by far the larger part of the premiums.

Frank was fun, every three weeks or so, but he was married and she knew that for him she was just fun too.

Jump over this possible yawning dark hole quickly. Done . . .

"You look funny. Are you catching a cold? Maybe you should stay home, go back to bed." Oh God, why had she said *back* to bed . . . ?

"Under no circumstances can I stay home. I am," Timmons said, getting up and leaving half his eggs and both pieces of toast, "going to be busy today. Very busy."

THREE

"Are you catching a cold or something?" Oliver asked. "You look a bit—incandescent."

Timmons had said, "Okay if we have coffee together before we get cracking?" and brought his paper cup and Danish into Oliver's cubicle. He looked with interest at Oliver's board, with the big white pad of paper on it. Package design, he couldn't tell for what, the lettering wasn't in yet, just the crisp broad purple and white stripes of the box, one of the stripes polka-dotted in purple.

"No, no cold. It must be nice to have interesting work to do."

"Nice enough," Oliver said, without a great deal of enthusiasm. Born in Paris, where his father had been in the diplomatic service, raised there and in New York, married and working and widowed in New York, he had taken a very dim view of moving with Bela from Manhattan to the wilds of New Jersey.

But jobs in his field were then particularly tight, and he was well paid, and a generous portion of each bi-monthly check went to his mother, in California. It went willingly; he was fond of his mother. The responsibility, however, didn't give him much choice; he had prepared to exile himself as cheerfully as he could in Jersey.

He was thirty-three, and a little above medium height. Sitting or standing, his body gave an impression of composure, ease in itself, coupled with a lithe waiting quicksilver strength. His hair was dun-colored and silky, and even when carelessly spilled invited, to women's hands, touching. His quiet forehead was finely turned at the temples, his nose high-bridged, his mouth aware and expressive. His hazel eyes were brilliant under angled thick brows.

Timmons had often thought it must be pleasant to be Oliver; to live inside that relaxed and ready body, inside those features, behind those perceptive eyes.

His company, now as always, was oddly reassuring. But energy was frothing up in Timmons as he finished his Danish. "I'll be off now. Lots of things to do."

"Me too," Oliver said. "A pill bottle is staring me in the face. Square shoulders, or round? Dark green glass or clear? As you pointed out, it's nice to have interesting work to do."

Timmons got himself to the bottom of the fourth and last page of the *Bela Beacon* with a much-padded account of the bowling tournament. It seemed to have happened very long ago.

Then he got out a lined yellow legal pad and cast his eye about the department. As though on cue, Veronica, at the desk in front of him, called, to the cubicle next to Oliver's, "I forget to tell you, Bob, your order came in this morning."

Robert Vander was the office manager of Section 4G, Packaging, Merchandising, and Sales Promotion. Among his other duties was authorizing and ordering supplies. A lot of people knew about his two daughters in art school and his way of providing for their expensive classroom needs by sandwiching them into his lists and charging them to Bela.

White Collar Crime, Timmons headlined to himself. Not a bad beginning, not bad at all.

Vander's mornings were predictable: coffee and a jelly doughnut and the Asbury Park *Press* until ten o'clock. His cubicle was glass from the belt up too, but his desk faced the wall, and he had, on moving in, placed a large obscuring sheet of paper on the glass on which was lettered:

THE LESS TALK THE MORE WORK. YOUR SILENCE IS A KINDNESS TO YOUR NEIGHBORS. COMPANY STATIONERY IS NOT TO BE USED FOR PERSONAL CORRESPONDENCE. PLEASE ANSWER TELEPHONES PROMPTLY, AND THAT MEANS NOT JUST YOUR OWN.

REMEMBER, WE'RE ALL ON THIS TEAM TOGETHER. THANK YOU. KEEP SMILING. ROBERT L. VANDER.

The sheet of paper made his little office an effective hiding place. He could even, if he wanted to, take a short refreshing nap after lunch.

Nine-forty-five now, by Timmons' watch. The medicine cabinet was in the mail room, so in case Vander for once abandoned his newspaper before ten, the aspirin bottle could be Timmons' goal there.

The mail room was empty. Toddy, the pleasant elderly man who was proprietor there would be delivering the morning mail to In boxes on two floors.

Oh, yes, quite a heap of packages for Robert Vander. Timmons zeroed in on the ones labeled Grumbacher. He was neat and quick with his penknife, slitting the heavy tape. Two dozen half-pound tubes of oil paint with names like Alizaran Crimson and Earth Green and Albumen White. Two dozen of the best oil brushes. Nobody in Section 4G used oils or brushes for anything. Oliver worked mostly with felt tips, occasionally dipping into precise and beautiful water color.

An expensive portable easel, with a matching folding stool. A dozen thick immaculate sheets of Watman board, far too costly for 4G use. Another cache of brushes, water-color brushes, sable-tipped, from hairline thin to plump. For Oliver? Oliver had a Delft mug which must have thirty brushes in it.

"Looking for something, Mr. Timmons?" Toddy asked, a foot behind him.

Timmons said vaguely, "Bob wanted me to check on . . . mmm . . ." Toddy wouldn't know or care; his question was a form of greeting. "While you're here, Toddy, would you mind getting me some stamps? Two fifteens, a twenty, and a four." The stamps were kept, under Toddy's care, in a small locked closet up the hall from the mail room. In the four minutes the stamp errand required—Toddy was not a man to rush himself—Timmons retaped the slit packages.

Back at his desk, he got to work on his yellow pad. Writing

away with his ball-point pen, he paused to gaze happily at Vander's cubicle.

(*Item #1. Robert L. Vander, Office Manager for Department 4G and also for Department 6D on the floor above, which you will know is Accounting and Billing, regularly orders supplies for his family's personal needs along with office materials. I believe this practice began about six years ago, shortly after he attained his position. A check today, 5/28, shows the following items not likely under any circumstances to be used in 4G:*) He totted up the items and prices conscientiously. (*Approximate cost of the above, $82.50. No doubt additional items of this nature will be ordered before this communication is submitted to you.*)

"What are you smiling about, Les?" Veronica asked, turning around to borrow a cigarette. She had almost, but not quite, given up smoking.

"It says on Bob's poster, keep smiling, doesn't it? I'm obeying orders," Timmons said.

Next he turned his attention to the matter of Marie Eggena. She had sprung into departmental prominence when, literally overnight the month before, she had been made Executive Assistant to Carl Ives, Copy Chief, Sales Promotion and Merchandising.

It was a new post, a created one. "I have to do a lot of running around, meetings away from the building, and so on," Ives explained to Personnel. "I need someone on top of things while I'm not there. Girl shows a remarkable executive ability and grasp of—of workflow." Ives and Brent were friends, and occasionally scratched each other's back.

Up to then, Marie Eggena hadn't seemed to show a remarkable ability for anything much. She wrote ads for trade publications, for Bela cosmetics and their hair products line; the consumer advertising, TV and print, was handled by a large

New York advertising agency. She was much given to doing her nails on company time. "Well, they *make* nail polish, so you might call it work," she would say when eyebrows were lifted. Her ideas were laboriously conceived, and not very good, and her copy sluggish and imitative.

But Ives had a soft spot for her, and took great trouble correcting her copy, juicing up her headlines, and explaining the intricacies of sales promotion to her. ("It's nice to earn while you learn," Veronica said.) She was very pretty, in her mid-twenties, with lavender-blond hair and matching huge tinted glasses.

A shock wave of surprise and resentment swept the department when she got her appointment and her new pale blue desk and matching chair in the cubicle next to Ives' real honest-to-goodness office.

It was generally and sourly concluded that she was sleeping with Carl Ives. Now this, as it stands, won't do me a great deal of good, Timmons thought. In his view the company probably didn't take a great deal of interest in its employees' morals. After all, Europeans—

Not a great deal of interest unless and until it interfered with the course of the day's business, when loose morals became money out of their pockets. The thing to do was catch her out in a few bird-brained decisions in Ives' absence, maybe touch on morale, better-qualified people passed by, people who had more to offer, dollars and cents, in the way of service and dedication.

Marie Eggena was not as it happened sleeping with Carl Ives, or not yet. One rainy night, he had spotted her, on the way to his car in one of the four immense parking lots of the Bela complex. She was standing dolefully under an umbrella beside an obviously locked and empty blue Pontiac.

"Stranded?" Ives asked.

"My ride's late, she may be another half hour, and . . ."

"Come with me, I'll drive you home, you're only a few

streets away from where I live." He was a dark thin dapper man with a mustache, well-dressed, carrying and even clutching to him a chestnut leather attaché case.

"Little drink on the way home?"

"I wouldn't mind. If it won't keep you late for dinner."

"Dinner is when *I* turn up and never before," Ives said, lordly. "There's this dark cozy place off the parkway at the next right."

The drink turned into a lot of drinks. Ives called home and said he'd be working late, don't hold dinner. Over some kind of hot sandwich, he discussed the color of her eyes, which he hadn't seen until now because of the big tinted glasses. Someone started to play the piano and they danced and had another drink or two.

They left the bar at twelve and Ives drove unsteadily homeward in the heavy rain. "Don't drop me in front of my house, my mother's got a gimlet eye, she wouldn't want to see me with a married man," Marie said blurrily.

"Okay, but how the hell she would know at midnight in the rain that I'm *married*—" Reaching for her thigh, his hand passed over a space on the seat where there should be something, something glossy and solid.

Swearing to himself, he stopped the car. Floor, back seat—nothing. He realized with an awful whack over the heart that he must have left his attaché case behind, at the bar.

He turned the car around with a small scream of rubber and she said, "What—?" looking suddenly frightened.

"Christ, I left my case, important papers in it, got to get it back—" and in the light from the dashboard she saw his face, wet, as if the rain had just hit it.

The attaché case held among other things a file on a top-secret new Bela heart medicine, referred to only, even in inner circles, as XX. He had been going to be a good boy, study it at home this evening, startle them with ideas on the new trade announcement campaign, which would be getting underway in two weeks. Sit in a meeting and say, as though he'd just thought it up, "Something just hit me. How about along these lines . . . ?"

He'd been told when reluctantly given the folder, "Guard this with your life, fella." When he left the building, the security man, checking his case, saw a number of file folders, this one being innocently labeled: "Rough notes for annual Twenty-Five Year Club dinner."

"Mr. Ives—Carl—I *can't,* it's late, I have to work tomorrow —"

"This only happens to be the most important thing in the world," he said, brushing sweat out of his eyes with a shaking hand and driving much too fast. Careful, might be arrested, and then—

The attaché case was nowhere to be found in the bar. "New looking, you say? Real leather? Could be someone picked it up thinking there might be some value in it," the manager-bartender said. "We've had a rough crowd in here tonight. God, Jersey's the living end. I wish I was back in Mineola."

There were other carbons in locked files, of course, but how was he going to explain the loss of this set? He had once covered up for Deering, the man who had given him the folder. Deering would just have to do a return favor. "Crazy kid of mine ran out of homework paper and used the backs of some of the sheets, I can't return them that way with an essay on Japan and arithmetic all over them—Don't worry, I flushed them down the toilet."

He drew a long sigh and started the car. Marie Eggena said, "For a little while there you looked like you were going to have a heart attack."

What a terrific story it would make over the girls' morning coffee and pastries. Driving like a madman . . . lost his attaché case, drinking . . . said it was the most important thing in the world . . .

It was too bad he hadn't dropped her, before going back to the bar. But every second had seemed to count. Still did. The morning, the workday morning, was not far away.

It was a product of panic, full of holes, but it would have to do, there wasn't time for something more careful, gradual. Forcing his voice to calm, he said, "Oh well, the hell with it . . . and, I know it's a funny hour of the night to talk about business, but our little party was in a way an advance celebration. I've been working on this . . . promotion for you. Didn't want to tell you in case it fell through, but I'll be announcing it in a day or so. Naturally, it wouldn't do to have anyone think we saw each other socially, not that that has anything to do with the job, but you know offices—"

He was talking so fast her head was spinning but the gist of it sounded good. Promotion? Why? For a moment suspicion licked at her and then her vanity took over, and burgeoned.

"Remember, not a word to anyone about this. About our—having a bit of fun, friendly—after working hours. Think of yourself as being part of the management team now. New job'll probably take one more day to go through. Act as if nothing's happened and then see me at say nine o'clock the day after. Friday. I'll drop you home now. Or rather a block away."

Slightly hung over, Marie sat dreamily apart from the girls, with her coffee. No point now in gossiping and giggling just like everyone else, and some of them were only secretaries, or even lower, typists. She pretended to be studying a trade journal. How delightful, hopping over the heads of Veronica Novach and Sally King and that snotty Mabel Kovarski, who'd been here since God made the world and was said to do twice as much work as anyone else, and who had been obviously slated for Ives' job when *he* was promoted. Or so they said.

Maybe in her new job she could from time to time *correct* Mabel's work, show her where she'd gone wrong . . .

The cubicle next to Ives' office had been empty. On Friday morning it was furnished with the new pale blue desk and chair, and tall white file cases, and a pot of philodendron wrapped in silver foil and satin-bowed in yellow.

Nervously, at 9:30, Ives used his personal click-in to the public address system. "Boys and girls, I have an announcement. As of this morning, Ms. Marie Eggena assumes the job, and the responsibilities, of executive assistant to yours truly. In other words, when I'm not here you'll see her, report to her, as you would to me, and of course accept assignments from her as you would from me. I know you'll all wish her well, and be cheered to see that rapid advancement is the middle name of department 4G. Thanks, and now"—a brief laugh—"back to work, or better still, finish your coffee. Cheers."

Marie Eggena rose demurely from her just-like-everybody's desk and walked princesslike into her new office. Two people clapped, there was a wolf-whistle, there was scowling, cursing, and over it all a persistent buzzing of voices.

Mabel Kovarski, quiet at her desk, smart in her black suit, forty years of age, olive-skinned and handsome in a bony saturnine way, stared at a sheet of paper in her typewriter through a haze of astonished tears. Her ears were ringing.

Before the real rage set in, her first surface reaction was, If that little bitch dares to set a finger on my work, I don't know what I'll do. I-do-not-know-what-I-will-do.

Make a start on this, Timmons thought, and then follow it up later, round it out. It looked fishy to say the least. It had to be promising.

(Item #2. A most amazing promotion in this section was announced today. A young girl, Marie Eggena, of little experience—2½ years—and no noticeable ability has been appointed executive assistant to Mr. Carl Ives, the department head. This in spite of the fact that Mr. Ives has highly trained and long-experienced staff members much more suited to assist him.)

He'd arrange an "interview" with her, Timmons decided. Invite her to lunch in the company cafeteria. Tell her he wanted to write her up for the *Bela Beacon.* Ask some searching questions with a straight face. He was glad he'd never lost his shorthand.

Ralph Horner, who was next in seniority to Mabel Kovarski, over Veronica and Sally, had thought the next step up was reserved for him. Okay, Mabel deserved it maybe. But Mabel was a woman and so not a major threat.

Brooding, he went out to lunch alone and had three double scotches and half a ham sandwich. He was a man with a sudden and violent temper, often an occasion of drama in 4G. He was given to throwing things on the floor, kicking wastebaskets, when his temper took over.

He came back after lunch and sat down at his desk and gave his typewriter table an almighty shove with a savage hand. It toppled over and the Remington electric went ominously, thunderously, crashing.

"Congratulations," he was heard to mutter, his face very red. And then, loudly, "Damned table, it had a loose joint, just trying to push it away for a bit of leg room . . ."

Ives was safely still out to lunch, and it was too early in the game to be frightened of that mindless whore Marie Eggena. The people around him would cover for him; management was no more beloved here than management anywhere.

(*Item #3. A sales promotion writer, Ralph Horner, who has been with the company for 14 years, has occasional bouts of ungovernable temper which he takes out on company property. Several months ago he kicked over and damaged a designer's drawing board in an argument about a display stand design.*) Oliver had, of course, won the argument hands down, but the edge of the board had cut his shin, right through his trousers and socks. (*On 4/25, he pushed over his typing table and his new Remington electric crashed to the floor. It must have been badly damaged as he is still using another machine.*)

FOUR

"Has Timmons been slugged over the head yet? Or perhaps a dash of poison in his coffee?" Louise Townsend asked.

"No, not yet," Oliver said. "I asked him if he'd put down anything good for today and he said yes, that the mashed potatoes in the cafeteria were watery."

"He could be putting up some kind of smoke screen," said shrewd Lou, idly though, amusement around her mouth echoing the expression of his.

They were stretched lazily on webbed plastic chairs under the big dogwood tree, which had long finished blooming at the side of the house. Late sun and shadow slanted across the lawn and caught itself deep in the ten-foot arborvitae nearby which had shaped itself into the semblance of an enormous Teddy bear.

A table between their chairs held a bowl of ice, a bottle of gin, two small half-empty bottles of tonic, and a saucer of limes. Courtesy of Oliver's landlady, this evening.

He had been delighted to stumble on 222 Lambert Road when he had been apartment hunting in late February. He had gazed with horror upon what were called garden apartments, with wall-to-wall carpeting and laundry rooms, mean small lots, cement walks, new-shoddy exteriors. And expensive at that, $220–$240 for a one-bedroom apartment, and you can supply your own heat in winter, thank you, run you about $35 a month. No, thank you. Of course Bela's moving in had sent rentals in all the towns surrounding Goodwood skyrocketing.

Two-twenty-two was an old white clapboard house, amply porched, Victorian and bay-windowed in front, colonial at the back, deep in its winter lawn under its great bare trees and its weeping spruces. He had been shown the upstairs apartment by a rental agent. Pleasant crooked arrangement, big living room, good-size bedroom, nice nameless small room that would provide an undreamed-of studio, modest, shabby kitchen with a small four-burner stove and nothing else. Planked oak floors throughout painted a soft pumpkin color.

In the kitchen, the rental agent said a little nervously, "I'm afraid you have to provide your own refrigerator. And the previous tenant took all his cabinets and stuff away."

"I'd provide *two* refrigerators," Oliver said happily. In his anxiety to get his hands on this place even before he asked what the rent was, he added, "I have no pets."

"Oh, pets are all right here."

"And no children," in a knee-jerk way, remembering the questions that had been put to him in those other, frightful places.

"Children would be no problem, Mr. Lee."

"What a nice old biddy my landlady must be," Oliver said.

"Oh, hardly old, Ms. Townsend . . ."

"How much?"

"Two fifty a month, all utilities, including heat." The agent waited tensely; the kitchen stopped most people, especially the women, in their tracks.

"Fine, when can I sign the lease?"

It turned out that, upon supplying credit and employment information, he could sign it right away.

His fish netted, the agent grew expansive, driving Oliver to the bus station. Oliver didn't own a car; living in New York, not given to country weekending, he didn't want or need one. He detested automobiles and wondered if now he'd have to join the enemy and buy one.

". . . an executive secretary in New York. The house is very old, back part of it dates back to the seventeen hundreds, somewhat modernized now of course. Her parents bought it years ago and handed it over to her. They live in Italy, although how, with all those strikes and Communists . . . Anyway, she occupies the ground-floor apartment, the back entrance through the winter porch is hers and you have exclusive use of the front entrance."

Oliver looked at his watch, half listening, mentally arranging furniture in his new quarters, but most importantly placing his easel and painter's clutter in the interesting small room facing, by some wild luck, north.

". . . lives in New York, uses the house on an occasional winter weekend, brings people down. And spring and summer weekends. Otherwise the place is mostly empty, all yours. Married and divorced, I'm told, but everybody seems to be these days . . ."

Oliver moved in early in April. No sign of his landlady, but her flowers, or her parents', were there, wide double borders on either side of the herringbone-brick front walk, tulips and daffodils, big heavy-headed hyacinths filling the air about them with a sweet yeasty smell, little grape hyacinths burning blue-purple, early frail purple and yellow iris.

On his first weekend he allowed himself to sit on the front steps of her porch and for his lunch drink a bottle of beer and eat bread and cheese. He had been painting since five o'clock in the morning and was floatingly pleased with everything, his beer, his cheese, the flowers, the play and shimmer of light in the band of woodland across the road.

It would be nice if they never showed up, ground-floor Ms. Townsend and her guests, laughter, voices, cook-outs? people sprawled all over the silent green lawn. Nice to have for his own the white solitude of the house.

"Oliver Lee," repeated his client over the telephone.

She had left to the real estate agent the discretion of taking on or refusing any particular tenant. "Good credit rating, not just a summer rental, works at that huge place, Bela, which has just moved here from New York. Respectable looking."

"Married?" Lou asked professionally. Wives hated the naked upstairs kitchen and would demand washer and drier, cabinets and new tiling on the floor. The house as now wired wouldn't take the extra demands on its hot water and electricity.

"I don't think so, he doesn't *look* married. There was nothing about, I have to wait until my wife looks it over. He took it in five minutes," the agent said.

Oh God, Lou thought; unmarried, parties, the old staunch house made to thump undignifiedly with hard rock, the stereo upstairs pumping, pounding, banging through the oak planks. The two young men the summer before, homosexuals; fine, okay, that was their affair, if they weren't right over your head. The quarrels, the noise—

One of them, the thin pale one, taking shelter, after a fight, in her winter porch, weeping. The other setting fire to their water bed, or trying to, in retribution, finally managing a tiny holocaust with the help of the bedside rug. The volunteer fire department of Farms River arriving in strength; a lost mad night when she had come down very tired just for a lazy day and night in summer.

But she should nevertheless be grateful for her new tenant Lee. The extra money came in handy and helped with the taxes. Take the best view of it, a girl up there with him, or several girls interchanged. The apartment had gone begging for ten months. It wasn't what people in New Jersey wanted. It was personal and old-fashioned and inconvenient.

On a day in May when she was driving down from her apartment in Chelsea to open up her own quarters—which meant flinging up windows and looking at the tulips, putting fresh sheets on her bed, telephoning her grocery and liquor store order—she began to muse with mild interest on the faceless being named Oliver Lee.

Shortly before turning off the Garden State Parkway, she passed her tenant's place of business, chaste huge white sign at the parkway's edge, BELA. No nonsense about Inc. or Ltd. At a discreet distance the complex of buildings loomed, sheathed in alabaster white, square-columned. A sort of new kind of Greek temples, she thought, but temples to money. The power of it, the immensity, reached out and gave its message to even the most casual passerby. The great tall poplars lining the drive to these mountains-of-the-moon structures must have been brought in, whole and adult.

("Great outside, if you like that kind of thing," Oliver told her later. "Maximum cheap inside. But as they make things you use in and on your body, the idea from the parkway is cleanliness and purity, and they do get away with it, don't you think?")

She turned into Lambert Road and, passing the housefront, saw a man, lithe and slender, on hands and knees, weeding one of the flower borders. He wore light-colored corduroy trousers and an orange-and-white seersucker shirt with the sleeves rolled up over his busy arms. The clarity of her mental photograph later surprised her: including the fact that the right-hand border had already been done, tidy brown ungrassed earth around the luminous leaves and flowers.

Left, up Jefferson Street, left again, to the short drive in back of the house. She got out of the car and went through the walled windowed porch to the ground floor apartment, alternately sun-flooded and blue-shadowed, all the east-facing windows a dazzle of pink and white dogwood.

Must do the proper thing. She went out, and around the house, to the front lawn. His back was to her.

"Good morning," she said to the trim corduroy rump. "I'm . . ."

He spun and got lightly and immediately to his feet.

". . . Louise Townsend."

"Oliver Lee." He extended a hand and then took it back, because it was covered with earth. "I'm delighted—with my apartment, I mean, and very nice to meet you."

"Thanks for weeding."

"You're welcome. I enjoy it."

To get off to an amiable start with the new tenant, she had brought down a bottle of chilled white wine, two lavish roast beef sandwiches, fruit and cheese. No matter what he's like, ask him to an al fresco lunch, she had thought, making the sandwiches.

Now she hesitated. She sensed at once that she must tread carefully, not come on as too sociable, intrusive, talkative, all over him, his peace and privacy shot to hell.

Open and direct as a rule, she stepped over her doubts. "It's lunchtime," she said. "I brought along some stuff to celebrate unloading the apartment after ten months. Will you . . . ?"

She had been right in her hesitation; she saw his own. Then he said politely, "If it's no trouble . . . and perhaps something we might eat on the front steps? I'm addicted to your steps, for lunch."

Maybe he would stare and refuse when she carried out the wine and the glasses. He didn't. He held his glass to the sunlight, gazed with pleasure at it, and took an inquiring sip. "Good," he said.

It was halfway through her pear and Brie that she decided that she must, absolutely must, have Oliver Lee.

All weekend she waited for the other shoe to drop, the pretty girl to drift down Oliver's inner stairway and appear on the lawn; or drive up and park in front of the house. Surely he didn't live alone?

No girl appeared. Away somewhere . . . ?

Having made her hospitable gesture, she left him to himself, trying to remember what she had come down here from New York to do. Oh, yes, sunbathe, and weed, but he'd taken over the weeding. Have dinner with old friends, the Tuckers. Get up early tomorrow and drive the six miles to the Atlantic, to what in New Jersey was called the Shore. Walk on the sand beside the morning sea, barefoot.

She applied herself to these diversions. He seemed to spend a great part of the weekend in his apartment. She wondered if he was hiding from her. Her Sunday afternoon sunbath went uninterrupted, close to the great green Teddy bear.

When, at seven, she went out to get into her car to drive

back to New York, he leaned out of his bedroom window and contentedly waved her good-bye.

They fell, neither pushing it, into an easygoing pattern of late-day drinks on Saturday. She asked him about Bela; the moon place intrigued her.

Bela had started, Oliver said, with pharmaceuticals, in Switzerland. "Now they own half the world, and make a hundred or a thousand things I won't bore you with, and pick up companies like someone eating peanuts. They run spas in Germany and the Caribbean. They have offices and plants all over Europe and South America, and here and Dallas, Mexico too I think. They remind me of an awful radio commercial from a few years back—'No matter where you go, you're never more than a foot away from somebody-or-other's product.'"

"And do you like it, what you do there?"

"Well enough," Oliver said serenely. "Do you like what you do, Lou?"

Odd. Her father called her Lou, and a few old close friends. It had come to be her own mental name for herself. The syllable fell naturally from his tongue after the first few weekends.

She felt she didn't look like a soft Louise. She was tallish, limber, leggy, vitality and a sort of gaiety about her like vividly moving air. She had a long rounded face, and slightly tilted long blue eyes given a merry look by the thrust of her cheekbones. Her straight swinging hair was cut in careless bangs, brown hair with childlike clean rose and blue gleams in the sunlight. The sun was on it now, dapplingly.

"Yes, very much. I don't run a very tight ship for myself, and it's in a way refreshing to run somebody else's working life with, if I say so myself, formidable efficiency. Besides, he's the president, so I have a front-row seat at the power game. It's entertaining in a blood-chilling way."

Bela led him one weekend in June to tell her about the man with fifty complaints.

When she asked him the question about Timmons being slugged over the head or poisoned, the other half of her mind was busy with, Private man that he is, maybe he doesn't like my knowing that someone lives here with him. Maybe she spends the five weekdays with him and then floats briefly away . . .

Oh, hell, take the gifts the gods provide, as her mother used to say. He was here at her side, relaxed, in his long chair, companionable, gently jingling ice-cubes in his drink.

He said, "That reminds me, he very ostentatiously hands me copies, in sealed envelopes. I just toss them in my desk drawer. I'm bad about remembering to lock things up, I must bring the batch home. And in case anything sinister happened to *me*, you'll find them, let's see, in my shirt drawer. And no doubt in your efficient way, Lou, you will proceed immediately to the proper authorities."

FIVE

It was on a Monday morning that Timmons made Oliver his unofficial trustee.

A small accidental crowd was around and near him, a new girl having coffee with Veronica, three men at the desk next to his making up some kind of baseball pool arrangement, Bob Vander passing by on the way to the water cooler.

Oliver was standing in his doorway. "Taking the air on my front stoop," he explained to Veronica. "I have a job waiting that lacks appeal."

Timmons raised his voice a little. "Oliver, here's a copy of my list to date, will you keep it for me? In case my original gets mislaid, or something."

"All right." Oliver accepted the long sealed white envelope and put it in his pocket. He was mildly amused at Timmons' playing cops and robbers, or Balkan spies, but it didn't show on his face. He transferred the envelope later to the drawer of the desk which stood at right angles to his board, and promptly forgot about it.

There was a little, interested silence and then the coffee-time chatter started again. The silence warmed and pleased Timmons.

His list was no longer a secret; he had been unable to resist dropping a few dark hints. Veronica summed up the general attitude. "Three complaints, big ones, okay. Five maybe. But fifty? Forget it. They'll flush it."

She was a blond woman in her early forties with a high-cheekboned Magyar face and observant sparkling dark eyes. Occasionally she teased Timmons about his list, but in a kindly fashion. She was fond of him after long acquaintance and sorry for him; she bet to herself his wife called the turn at home. "Hey, Les, in case you can't get all the way up to fifty, three of the soap dispensers in the ladies' room were empty last week. Of course you'd have to change it to the men's room, but they must get empty too sometimes."

And, "I would and yet I wouldn't want to see your list, Les. I suppose you're naming names?" "Of course I'm naming names." "Aren't you," chuckling, "afraid?" "What, afraid to practice my rights as a free citizen and employee?"

Oliver heard this exchange. From his cubicle, he said, "Damn the torpedoes."

Timmons suspected that they were laughing at him behind his back. Their derision didn't bother him at all. He was nourished and sustained by the project, and there was a new flavor on his palate, the taste of power.

The list never left his person. At night, after dinner, he would sit at the card table by the window in the living room, next to Lara's cactus collection on the sill, annotating, studying, cherishing it.

Once Lara said, "What's that work you have? At what they pay *you*, take-home work yet!"

"They're thinking of making the *Beacon* a weekly and God knows how I'll be able to fill it," Timmons explained vaguely. "I've got to be ready with items."

He had never told her the flat-out truth about being more or less permanently refused a raise. It was kind of fuel that helped to keep him running, and he didn't want to diffuse it by sharing it. He had almost erased from his immediate consciousness the other catalyst, that night with Lara and Frank Rainer. After all, he had been dignified about it.

"It's of no consequence to me," he had said. He had had the last word.

Touching upon his interview, he reported, "Be patient, Lester. That's what Kalish told me. And that some of the raises that have gone through were scheduled from a year ago and it will take a while to process mine, what with the expenses of moving."

"Patient, patient—be patient won't pay the gas and electric or the telephone or the groceries." But, aware of an odd new firmness about him, and still feeling guilty about the trick she had played on him with Frank, she dropped it for a while.

There were a few people who were not particularly amused by Timmons' list.

Charlie Corleone came in and stood over Oliver's drawing board. "You're within spitting distance of him, you ought to know . . . what is he, some kind of nut?"

And what was *he* worried about, Oliver thought idly, theft, drink, women on the side, or song? (Corleone sang Italian arias to himself, in the men's room, and could be heard offices away. This guy's really had it, people said. I mean, at the top of his *lungs*.)

"Yes, I suppose he's a nut, about this one thing—to use the term loosely. But then so are a lot of people who sit in airport control towers and run armies and multinational companies. And governments." Sprawled all over his pad were different styles of lettering and script for Bela's new perfume, Yours Truly. He picked up a felt-tipped pen and set the name down in typewriter typeface, and said to himself consideringly, "I don't think so . . ."

"I say he's looking for trouble one way or another. The poor bastard . . ." But there was no compunction whatever in his voice.

Oliver suffered an unseen wince. Poor bastard, words so painfully accurate applied to Timmons that he never even allowed himself to use them mentally.

"Someone said he gives *you* duplicates in case his desk is robbed . . ."

Oliver did Yours Truly in a loose dancing script, which he decided he liked. "I dropped my scout's honor and slit one of them open," he said as if to himself, without any sound of invention in his voice. "Blank paper, a bluff. You sing, he complains, everybody has a right to his own quirk."

Later that week Timmons found to his great pleasure that his desk drawers had been searched at some time between five last night and 9:05 this morning.

He had for several weeks been deliberately leaving the desk unlocked.

A neat enough job, you'd never guess at the probing, prying fingers from the look of his filing drawers full of manila folders holding carbons of his copy for the medical brochures, and back issues of the *Bela Beacon*.

The center drawer held the usual litter of pencils, paper clips, rubber bands, erasers, extra sugar packets, stapler and small scratch pads. It looked all right too, except that the fingers had replaced the stack of four pads at the *right* side of the drawer, instead of the left.

"Veronica," he murmured to the busy red-wool back at the next desk up. She swiveled from the desk to her typewriter and put in a sheet of yellow paper.

"Arthritis, I'm sick to death of arthritis, I've been two weeks on this job and I swear my knuckles are growing knobbier every day and there's a twinge in my thumb joint . . . yes, Les?"

"You get in early. Did you see anyone around my desk?" Stretching out the enjoyment, the little triumph.

They could laugh, but someone was worried, someone was afraid.

"No, not a soul, why? You haven't been—?"

"Not robbed as far as I know, but yes, the desk has been searched. Very thoroughly searched."

Veronica was wide-eyed for a moment; then she grinned. "Maybe I'd better have my desk position switched, you're a dangerous man to be next to, with your poison-pen papers . . ." He saw that she was excited and refreshed by this little diversion from her arthritis brochure.

"Keep your ears open."

"I will, I will, you never know what you're going to pick up in the ladies' room. It would make *you* blush sometimes, Les."

She typed, "After fifteen years of testing, Ar-X has proven itself an eminently . . ." Her fingers stopped. "Of course, you wouldn't leave it lying around, I mean it would make me a little nervous if you did."

"Under no circumstances," Timmons assured her.

Two days later he got a sheet of lined legal-size yellow paper in his In box, folded in three and paper clip-fastened. He opened it and read the typed words, "You'd better tear that list up and forget it, you rotten spying little shit, or you'll regret it, and I mean REGRET it."

Unsigned, sexless, it could be male or female. He could check all the typewriters to see if he could spot the right one, but he had an idea that the massive electrics were efficiently uniform and didn't offer the minutely different characteristics of the manual machines.

It didn't matter. Whoever had written it had something to hide, and was either already on the list or would be, never fear. Handling it very carefully he tucked it into his wallet. A faint pleasurable tingle touched his spine. Someday, in case someone should try something, the police would probably want to dust it for fingerprints . . .

He got up early the next morning, and using an old bottle of Bela Bewitch, discarded by Lara after she had gone brown, dyed his thin hair a brown-blond, not, he thought, unlike Oliver's color. He dressed carefully, and found a bow tie he hadn't worn for years, quite clean, navy-and-white polka dots. He liked a bow tie, he felt jaunty wearing one.

At breakfast, Lara demanded, "What are you doing in your good suit? Big meeting? Is someone giving a banquet for you?"

"It never hurts to present a good appearance," he said. "And what am I saving it for? We haven't gotten to the age when we have friends' funerals piling up, and not that many people at our age get married either."

Leaning against the counter, munching her toast, she stared at him. Something new she couldn't put her finger on, a liveliness, looking pleased with himself, a fresh scrubbed pink to his face. He looked younger and his stoop seemed to have disappeared. Whatever it was, she resented it, holding that there was nothing here in Goodwood to be pleased about.

Still no raise, and the toilet had broken yesterday—in a new house, for God's sake—and she'd expected to hear from Frank a week ago and hadn't. And the scale this morning had told her she'd put on nine pounds, have to cut down on the beer, but what else was there to amuse yourself with, nights, in this nowhere Jersey town?

As an afterthought, she accused, "You dyed your hair."

He stroked it complacently. "Should've done it long ago."

An awful thought struck her. A woman, a girl, at work? That would explain the clothes, the excited color, the dye job. He'd never as far as she'd known shown any interest in other women. Fear and chill followed close behind the thought. Les wasn't like that, or hadn't been. Les was a permanent, always-there kind of man, kind of husband.

She looked down at her old blue-and-orange kimono, a birthday present from him three years back, and saw the bulge of her stomach, a coffee stain on the tail of a dragon, and below, the scuffed mauve-colored mules, dingy at the toes.

He got up from the table and patted his breast pocket, which now that she remembered he had taken to doing every morning.

"That apple I had yesterday was so sour it hurt behind my ears. Don't you have any decent fruit in the house? This time of year the peaches ought to be coming in."

"You don't have to be rude about it," she said in a hurt and somehow humbled voice. "Yes, I bought peaches yesterday. I won't even tell you the price, you'd choke on them." She put two peaches in his brown paper bag.

He kissed her a light good-bye and went happily off to work.

There were a few intent glances at his new-colored hair, and Jim Beadon grinned and said, "Someone got struck young during the night," but that was all. Hair dye, usually ineptly applied, was now a commonplace among the older Bela men.

At twelve, Timmons asked Veronica if she'd like to go to lunch with him, to the Ginger Inn. He had thought all morning how nice she looked today, navy trousers suit, crisp white shirt, hair ruffled brightly from running her hand through it while she worked.

He noticed and read her slight hesitation before she said kindly, "I'd love to, Les, but this is D-Day for arthritis, I'm going to get it out by five if it kills me. I'll be typing between bites of my cucumber sandwich."

His interpretation of her refusal, as gratifying or more so than an acceptance, was that she didn't want to be seen privately lunching with him, gossiping over a drink and a sandwich, by fellow workers. In case they might think he was telling her some of the things he had found out and put down on paper. From Odds-and-ends Man, he had gone on to Possibly Dangerous Man.

In the ladies' room, as they repaired their lipstick after lunch in front of the wide mirror, Veronica said to Bess Murphy, "I felt bad about saying no. I'm sorry for him. He's never invited me to lunch before. But somebody searched his desk, and yesterday he got what I think was some kind of nasty note. He just sat and stared at it and his face looked funny . . . You have to be careful about what you get into. Remember last year when that man in R and D up and shot his wife dead? Over the Fourth of July, it was."

There was no Oliver to have a drink and lunch with; he was imprisoned in a day-long meeting at the advertising agency in New York. He hated such meetings. "Approximately six hours to decide whether—to begin with—the label should be in a circle, or an oval, or an oblong, or a square. Nobody really talking about the label, you understand, but talking about them*selves*."

Luxuriously, and for the first time, Timmons allowed himself to think, about trapped Oliver, the poor bastard . . .

Once a week, as a democratic gesture toward the staff, the two personnel men, Brent and Kalish, ate lunch in the company cafeteria.

They picked up plates of today's special, stuffed peppers with tomato sauce, and rolls and butter, and apple pie for Brent, who naturally preceded Kalish in the line, raspberry pudding topped with fake whipped cream for Kalish.

As befitted men with confidential matters to discuss, they chose a corner table in a thinly populated part of the cafeteria and applied themselves efficiently to their food.

Having demolished his stuffed pepper, Brent said, "This business of Timmons . . ." and waited, with the air of one descending with distaste to minor matters.

Kalish buttered his poppy-seed roll. "The simplest thing to do would be to fire him."

"That wouldn't stop him sending off his preposterous document. And it would merely lend credence to whatever arrant nonsense he's put down." Brent had taken a course in Executive Profile and had learned how to discard short simple words.

"Well, frame him and fire him, then," Kalish said. "God, these rolls are hard. Put something in his desk. A memo, secret, about the new toothpaste or something. Of course, not the correct specifications. Idea being that he was going to sell it to interested people outside Bela."

"He's been with us for twenty-five years. Excellent record in a small way. Dedicated worker and doesn't, as far as we know, thieve. His associates might tend to be suspicious. I'm sure his list is common knowledge. Cat among the pigeons. Morale tottering . . ."

"I'm told he gives copies, or carbons, or whatever, to Oliver Lee, in case somebody swipes his. Or if anything"—Kalish grinned over his coffee cup—"crazy as it sounds, happens to him. At least that's the way Rosalie passed it on to me."

"Well, you might have a little chat with Lee, man to man, but don't get his back up, antagonize him rather, he's good and the big boys at Thompson are impressed with him. Mind getting us both another cup of coffee?"

Kalish did mind, but comforted himself with the thought that sooner or later he would be able to give the same order-request to *his* assistant. Brent, he knew, already had one foot in the door of top management in Bela Building Number One, with columns not just in front but on all four sides.

(*Item #39. Harold Brent, personnel manager for Buildings Two through Eight, is having an affair with the wife of Kingman Cone, President, Mycroft Pharmaceutical, a neighboring company but as you know a strong U.S. rival, near Lakehurst, N.J.*) This he had gotten from Lara, on the receiving end of a long chain of gossip started by Mrs. Cone's maid, who added that Mr. Cone was no angel either. "Honest to God!" Lara had said. "Kind of an unofficial merger!" (*This seems to me a potentially dangerous association from the business point of view.*)

SIX

It was a Friday afternoon in July. The usual lighthearted lassitude had spread through the office. People made working gestures but were not really working hard. I'll put that off till Monday morning, why start on a Friday? Soon they would scatter to their weekends, the Shore, the action-packed boardwalk at Seaside Park, back-yard swimming pools, crabgrass-battling, fishing off Barnegat Light, drinking beer and watching baseball on TV.

"What do you do with your weekends?" Timmons had once asked Oliver. He was sure it was none of these things.

"Paint, mostly," Oliver said.

"I'd love to see a painting of yours sometime," wistfully.

"We'll arrange it," Oliver said in a pleasant uncommitting way.

At quarter to five, he was already gone. Few of the cubicles and offices were occupied by now. The pool eliminated even working gestures and sat chatting. Vander was still in there, behind his poster.

Timmons had, between 3:30 and 4:30, been working away at his lined yellow pad. He was watched, and knew it.

Ostentatiously, he would start a sheet and continue, then study it, frown at it, and impatiently tear it off the pad, crumple it up, and toss it into his wastebasket. Giving the impression that the phrasing, the facts, weren't exactly the way he wanted them. Starting fresh, frowning and absorbed, after each crumple.

He was simply amusing himself. It would be nice to know who had searched his desk, a little fish or a big one.

People would tell people, word would sift through 4G. Timmons is at it again. And heaving stuff into his basket. The basket might hold an intense interest for someone, and very soon.

Vander left exactly at five. Timmons left one minute later. He was the last person in the great empty space that smelled of cigarette smoke and male and female scents, the closest and strongest being Veronica's Lovestorm, disloyally worn; it was a product of Mycroft Beauty Laboratories. The cleaning people, he knew from occasional night work, wouldn't be in until seven.

He went down in the elevator to the entrance lobby, where splendor briefly showed itself before vanishing completely. Pale pink marble wall facing, floor to match, a fountain leaping in a pool surrounded with tubs of ivy and red and white and pink geraniums. The security guard at the door yawned and said, "I s'pose you haven't any secret formulas in your pocket?—Coming on for rain. Have a nice weekend, Mr. Timmons."

Timmons drove a half mile. The guard had been right, heavy rain started, but he would have turned back anyway. A forgotten library book was his backup excuse.

To the guard, he said, "Left my rubbers and raincoat in there."

As he looked very much like a man who would not only wear rubbers but who would forget them, and forget his raincoat, the guard admitted him amiably.

Timmons didn't take the elevator up. It made a little, arriving *chunk* when it reached its signaled floor. He climbed the steps instead.

The stairway gave on a long corridor of mean proportions, identical to the four above it, thinly floored with plastic tile that Oliver had described as slime-green, over mercilessly hard concrete. Facing him was the shorter passage into 4G, coat closets on both sides, with gray-painted panels, already a little warped, that opened out in V's. When he was several feet away from the passage's end, Timmons thought he heard a small and very secret sound.

The pool had windows on one wall and offices and cubicles around three. Rain darkened the windows. There were no lights on, only the spent-breath illumination of the 40-watt bulbs at either end of the outer corridor.

With infinite caution, Timmons moved to the wall, then to the edge of the pool, where the floor became slime-green patterned with alternating squares of, Oliver said, bull's-blood red.

The sound hadn't after all been connected with rummaging in his wastebasket.

Her back was to him. Mabel Kovarski's straight, strict back. She must have been in the ladies' room when he left, thinking himself the last one there.

She was in Marie Eggena's cubicle. Doing—what?

It was like television with the sound turned off. Swiftly, violently, silently, she went about what she was doing.

At any minute she might turn around and see him. He slipped to the nearest desk, got down behind it—the row of eight desks in front would hide him—and peered over the edge. He turned his head for a second to check; there wasn't a window directly behind him to silhouette him from the eyes up.

Because of the glass beginning at waist height, he had to interpret the conclusion of each action from the starting motions visible through the glass. But that wasn't difficult. The white drawers of the filing cabinets, now; she was gently pulling them out—odd, the gloves on her hands in July—and slowly turning them upside down. Then the cabinets themselves were tilted and lowered out of sight.

She turned and seemed to look directly at him. She was smiling, and from a certain lift and fall of her shoulders appeared to be breathing hard, panting. She lifted a white paper cup of something dark, coffee, and stood spilling it. On the contents of the filing drawers, probably.

The savagery of her smiling face terrified him. Hard-working, conscientious Mabel. No laughing, talking, idling for her.

Marie had a set of blue-painted shelves with her philodendron on top, still satin-bowed and wearing its silver foil. With her strong hands, Mabel uprooted the plant and tossed it to the floor, and then dumped the contents of the large pot onto the desk. One busily moving arm suggested she was spreading the earth.

What was that in her hand now? An ink bottle. She must have gotten it from Oliver's supplies, the rest of them used ball points on which was imprinted, "Above All Bela."

She poured and flung it, generously, spinningly. Some of it splashed the glass.

Timmons cast his mind back over the day. He hadn't noticed any encounter between Mabel and Marie. *That* had been last week. Veronica had reported it to him.

"Couldn't wait to get her whacks in at Mabel. Remember, Mabel used to correct *her* stuff when Ives wasn't here to do it. Well, Josie sits right by Marie's door, and it was open, and she heard Marie saying to Mabel, 'I think you've got the wrong slant on this. You've put the most important thing last and the least important thing first, like Mr. Ives used to tell me when I was a beginner, but of course you're—anyway, let's try a rewrite.' And I mean, Les, in January Mabel got a prize, a *national* prize, for the best trade campaign of the year . . ."

Of course. Good strategy on her part to hold in her fury, let a week go by, and then there would be no immediate connection between her and the destruction. As a matter of fact, Marie and Ralph Horner had had a loud difference of opinion this afternoon when she tried to assign him a job he thought beneath him.

"I'm damned if I'll do it," he had shouted. "Get someone else to shovel that particular pile of manure," and he had walked red-faced with rage from her office and crashingly kicked his wastebasket over.

Marie had given the job he spurned to Mabel, who had calmly accepted it and finished it in fifteen minutes. Supermarket and drugstore shelf streamers for the annual fall sale of Bela Formula 100 Cough Syrup, buy two bottles, get one at half price.

Now she was pulling down the travel posters taped to the back wall,

WALK INTO HISTORY IN WALES, COME PUB WITH US IN BRITAIN, SUNNY SPAIN BECKONS YOU.

Faint crumpling, tearing noises.

She paused and with a long visible sigh looked around her and down at the floor, and she smiled again.

Then she moved to the closed door of the cubicle. Timmons squeezed himself ignominiously under the desk, not able to hear her footsteps over the pounding of his heart. She'd have to pass right by him.

She did. There was the sound of a closet panel V-ing open, the rustle of a raincoat being put on. His heart calming, he could hear better now. Almost silent footsteps going across into the corridor, and, not down the steps, but up. To Accounting and Billing. What, eventually, would she do about the guards, front *and* back?

From long ago, a memory surfaced. They had found themselves at the same table in the cafeteria and had fallen into conversation. Timmons was complaining about having had to work late the night before.

She said, "And because we're supposed to be classy white-collar, no overtime." She was known to be the stay and support of an ailing father. "And with me, it's a double problem, I always wake Dad up when I come in no matter how quiet I am. So when it's really late, and this is just between us, I sleep on the sofa in the ladies' room, and get up early, and get to my desk . . . I won't say it's the most comfortable way to spend the night, but it saves *him*."

Rubbered and raincoated, he took the elevator down, waved his hand at the guard and, crossing the parking lot to his car, was torn. He liked her. She was in a way too strong to be sorry for, but he was sorry for her anyway. What he had seen was something no one ought to be allowed to see. A kind of killing, but with no body to have to answer for.

But it was too good, too real, too finally provable—helping to authenticate the rest of his list—to pass up.

Your job is not to play favorites, he reminded himself. But to report, report exactly what's going on at Bela-Goodwood.

When he got home, he said to Lara, "Is there any liquor in the house?"

"A little Four Roses, why?"

"Let's have a drink. It's Friday. You fix it, will you? I have a thing for the *Beacon* I have to put down before I forget the details."

Back in May, he had said something to her about his projected line-up of complaints to be sent to the head office in Switzerland. She had said, "For God's sake, you'll get yourself fired, that's all you need, thrown out on your ass," and after that he had kept it to himself, at home.

With a hand still unwilling, slow, stiff, he wrote:

Item #40. On 7/17, after closing time, Mabel Kovarski, senior copywriter, entered the office of Marie Eggena, Executive Assistant to Carl Ives, and . . .

"Here's your booze, Les," Lara said, putting the glass down beside his pad. He flipped the top page over hastily. "Cheers."

"Cheers," Timmons said, drinking. Maybe the liquor hadn't been such a good idea; it burned his throat and he fell into a coughing spell.

"Some drinker you are," Lara said, laughing. "Here, I'll thump your back for you."

The cleaning crew came in at seven. A woman named Angela Oriano shrieked when she saw the disaster that had struck Marie Eggena's cubicle. She blessed herself and muttered something about devils and told the head man, Mr. Gotway, about it.

The guard at the front and back entrances had just finished

duty; the night watchman would be in charge until eight A.M. He shook his head at the damage. "Like somebody tried to kill somebody, but no blood—just ink and dirt and coffee." He searched the entire floor and then boldly went into the ladies' room. Empty, silent; smells that pleased him, face make-up and perfume. Lipsticked pieces of paper toweling in the large wire wastebasket.

He put a padlock on Marie Eggena's door, after ordering that none of the mess within be touched. "Police matter, probably," he said, exhilarated, "after the Security Head takes a look. But he's in Montreal for his mother's funeral. Won't be back till Sunday night."

Mabel Kovarski slept, on and off, during the night, in Accounting and Billing, stretched out on the clean daybed required by law in ladies' rooms for the comfort of female employees with possible monthly cramps or allied indispositions.

At nine in the morning, she called her father; he would be awake now.

"I went to a shower, a kitchen shower, didn't want to wake you, so I came over here, to Jessie's in Bayside. See you soon."

This would cover the remote chance that someone might ask her father if she had come home at the usual time, Friday night. It had in a way been worth it; she felt cleansed and peculiarly exhausted, empty. But if it ever came out . . . don't think about that. Because it would be as eventually final as slashing her own throat. She would be put down as unemployable at the very least, and mad, at the most likely.

If anyone attracted immediate blame, it would probably be Ralph Horner, with his blazing tempers. She would have cared about that once, but she didn't any more. He thought he was next in line to Ives. Walking hobnailed over her prone hurting body.

She fixed her face and hair and went out the back way, a good half hour before the Saturday mail would be delivered. There was no guard on the rear entrance on weekends. She walked perhaps a quarter of a mile, skirting the silent buildings. An occasional car parked here and there, the obsessed people who, as she often did, had to prove something by working on weekends; or who couldn't stand it at home, the children and all that, and fled to the office and made up things with which to occupy themselves. She had never used, in her car or on foot, Exit B, at the northern end of the Bela complex, the driveway bordered with impatiens, red, pink and white, the Bela flag colors.

The guard at the gate, already bored and already fortified with two cans of beer, looked at her inquiringly. "Sorensen," she said. "Building number seven." Her dark glasses were opaque, her head scarf muffling, her clothes neat and unmemorable.

"Okay, miss, nice weekend for those who *have* a weekend." The dark glasses were looking past him, to where the sun blindingly struck a newly opened beer can in his little sentry lodge.

"Thanks."

Later, when questioned, he said, No, nobody had gone out Exit B Friday night or Saturday morning. Just in case Dark Glasses, questioned in her turn, might bitch about his peaceful morning beer.

Monday morning fueled 4G with enough excitement and pleasure to last at least two days.

Marie Eggena, beholding the ruin that had once been her honored private place, fell first into obscenities that surprised a few people and then into hysterics, and had to be taken sobbing by Ives to the Medical Station three floors above in R and D, where she was given a sedative and commanded to, in Nurse Givens' words, "lay down."

There was a great commotion of guards, including the head. Vander as office manager presided. Questions were asked, work delightfully disrupted.

It emerged that Timmons had come back Friday night for his rubbers and raincoat. He answered the guards with the assurance of innocence:

"*I* had nothing to do with any of that. I just put on my rubbers and then I had to go to the men's room . . . I've had this virus and . . . Yes, I was up here ten minutes, thirteen, maybe. I wouldn't wish this virus on *you* . . . No, I didn't see a soul."

From far across the room, where it must have been impossible to hear what he was saying to Vander and the guards, Mabel Kovarski turned her thinned dark golden eyes on him, and for a moment he was frightened. For reassurance, he patted his breast pocket.

SEVEN

Timmons had several cronies who, far from deriding his list, occasionally gave him material for it, things he himself had no way of knowing about. Helpful: the broader the picture, he thought, the better.

From Consumer Overview, a long-established but newly named section (Brent's idea) in the sprawl of Research and Development, Mary Cleary called him, on a Tuesday that threatened thunderstorms later in the day.

"Like to bring your morning coffee up here? Something interesting."

She was one of two Overview supervisors, a plain, nice, heavily freckled woman in her mid-forties. The staff, mostly young, often only worked for a few weeks to pick up beach and beer and surfing money. They spent their days plodding from door to door handing out new Bela products in various stages of development and returning after the home trial with long questionnaires. Or, with no products involved, they were required to have what Overview called deep interviews with the consumer. What *didn't* they like about their present toothpaste? mouthwash? shampoo? hair coloring? aspirin product? If they had their way, how would they like the given product to work?

"Have a piece of apple cake, I made it myself," Mary Cleary said. "Guaranteed digestible, I know you and your innards. *Well!*" Her eyes were alight with enjoyment. "I know Ron Kalish is no favorite of yours . . ."

"Not exactly," Timmons said eagerly. Kalish, who had really started the whole thing; Kalish, buzzing around in his head, that night in the garage when he was curled up under his raincoat on the back seat of the car.

It emerged that Kalish had hired a new interviewer at the top salary allowed for the work. Blunt, Mary said, "You ought to see him. A very beautiful kid. Eyelashes out to here. A sort of . . . boardwalk version of a Greek god. Bronzed and all that. I gave him a job to do and he hadn't a clue how to go about it, and I ask you, *top* salary, only fifteen dollars less per week than *I'm* making."

She paused for a sip of coffee. "Don't write anything down here, Les, people will think I'm telling you tales out of school, you're a celebrity in a way up here now, did you know that?—Anyway, I had an extra day's vacation coming so yesterday I took a run down to Stone Harbor to my sister's. I was walking on the beach for some air and who do you think was lounging behind the dunes, up at the empty end?—Kalish and this kid, in sort of man-bikini shorts or trunks or whatever you call them. Looking quite, excuse the expression, attached to each other. And he, the boy, was supposed to be out on a full day's work, follow-up questionnaires on Placquemaster toothpaste."

"Very foolish," Timmons said, delighted. "Where's the boy today, and what's his name? And is Kalish on vacation?"

"On the beach, for all I know. Some of them are good at filling in their own questionnaires, faking it, but it takes a little practice . . . and I can usually spot it, anyway. Just let me get my hands on his when he finally coughs them up. His name is Gordon Forley. And, no, Kalish isn't on vacation. I called Rosalie and she said he'd had to fly out to the Dallas plant Sunday night and wouldn't be back till tomrorow."

Feeling a little like a private eye, he asked tightly, "Did Kalish—did they see you?"

"No, I don't think so. Too interested in each other, and I was on the dunes above. Of course, Stone Harbor's almost a hundred miles from here, but still, I call that living dangerously."

Timmons finished his coffee. For both of them, he put a decent face on the conversation. "God, when you think how hard we work, *have* worked, all these years, nose to the grindstone, Bela Above All . . ."

"Exactly," Mary Cleary said. "In our day we weren't taught how to play, at work. Maybe we missed out on something, Les."

"The storm will break," Veronica prophesied to Oliver, "just when we go out the door to the parking lot. Les must have gotten something good today, he has that pink look, like somebody turned on an electric light inside him."

Oliver said, "You're like a Greek chorus, Veronica."

She looked puzzled. "I'm not Greek, and I can't even carry a tune . . . but just you wait, five o'clock on the dot."

It turned out that Oliver didn't have to buy a car after all. A man named Lamb had bought a house on the river, a long wandering block south of 222 Lambert Road. He offered Oliver a regular ride; known to have no car and no television set, Oliver was regarded as something of an enigma by normal red-blooded car-addicted Bela males.

Oliver said yes, thanks, and paid over Lamb's protest for his share of the gas, once every two weeks. Not a man who enjoyed supermarkets and carts, he ordered most of his groceries by telephone, another habit of his considered exotic. When he ran out of something unexpectedly, he either walked or bicycled to the A&P a mile away on Route 37, borrowing Lou's bicycle, which she kept on the side porch. "A *girl's* bicycle?" Lamb had asked, eyebrows flying high. "Why not? It has two wheels and pedals."

Lamb, misnamed, was a big, bull-chested man, a chemist in R and D. He was rumored to keep a bottle in his desk drawer, and often allowed himself long liquid lunch hours. It was an understood thing that when he was, at the end of the day, a little blurred, a little high-colored around cheeks and chin, Oliver would drive, drop him and the Buick at the house by the river, and walk home. He would say, "My eyes are giving

me a bit of trouble, too much close work . . . will you . . . ?"
"Yes, okay, John," Oliver would say.

Lamb came by at 5:10, very flushed this evening. Veronica had been wrong; the rain hadn't yet started, but the western sky outside was an intense purple. Mine the wheel, Oliver thought, picking up his raincoat.

In the parking lot, Lamb said nothing about his eyes but got determinedly into the driver's seat.

"Sure you're all right to drive?" Oliver asked forthrightly.

There was something secretly, heavily belligerent about the usually affable Lamb. "Of course I'm all right to drive. Mind if I stop and do a quick errand on the way home?"

Thunder whispered its coming might at them. The purple in the west began to shroud the sky overhead.

"I'm in no position to mind," Oliver said, and added to himself, I'll pray my way home.

Lamb took the Buick down Goodwood Boulevard at moderate speed, turned east on Route 37, and drove what seemed to Oliver an interminable distance through the dark grim landscape. A huge bank, looking lost in its grassy lawns, it ought to be in a city; a mortician's comfortable shuttered clapboard last home for one's beloveds. Fruit and vegetable stands charging exorbitant highway prices to the naïve people who thought you got a bargain at these stands. Gas stations, used car lots, festooned with high wires dripping ribbons of gold foil that swam in the gathering wind. A clutter of restaurants, where everything would be deep-fried or drowned in mayonnaise. A frightful cemetery with, instead of gravestones, plastic baskets of plastic flowers used as markers for the interred bodies. That's Uncle Joe, the peach gladiolas.

Christ, Oliver thought—almost neurotically responsive to his immediate surroundings—just for the moment I wish I were dead.

The car swerved slightly. "Sorry," Lamb said, a little thickly.

Up ahead was a log-cabin looking building with a red neon sign proclaiming a brand of beer.

"I'm thirsty, let me off on the right, will you?" Oliver said. "For some reason I'm not in the mood for errands, anybody's. I'll call a taxi to take me home, from wherever in God's name we are."

"No, I won't," Lamb said. "It's not far from here . . ."

He drove over a long bridge, with the beginnings of a littery lot of shore houses, close together, bald burned lawns, cracked sandy sidewalks, to the right. He turned left, went up a narrow asphalt road between low scrub now wind-wracked, and left again, up a sandy track in the dunes, the Atlantic waking, heaving, angry, seventy feet away and down from them. He stopped the car.

"Now we can have our talk," he said. "I thought some place private would be best."

Three great drops of rain hit the windshield with the impact of flung coins. In the mauve flare of lightning, Lamb looked to Oliver like a heavy in an old movie, solid, menacing, his face in this light more purple than red.

"Talk about what?" But he knew right away.

"That shit list of Timmons'. You have copies. Someone told me about that."

Unintimidated at the moment, Oliver said, "And–?"

Lamb reached across him with a loop of keys. He unlocked the dashboard compartment. In it, a visual shock, was a greasily gleaming black handgun.

"Just wanted to get my spare pack of cigarettes. Nice little job, that–isn't it? I got mugged last year in a parking lot. Once is too often to do anything to yours truly. Next time I'll say, okay, okay, I keep my wallet in the dashboard, and then –whammo."

He lit a cigarette. "I suppose you've read the whole works."

"No. I already know more about my cohorts than I ever wanted to. What's your problem? Being scolded for late lunches?" The second half of the question was lost in an overhead crash of thunder that seemed to rock the car.

". . . had me on the carpet," Lamb now could be heard to say. "*Me.* After fifteen years, and I was the one who dreamed up the mouthwash, they've made millions out of it. Next thing, I suppose, no-smoking signs in the men's room."

He swung sideways and embarrassingly clapped Oliver on the shoulder.

"Look, pal, all I'm asking is has he put me down on his list, and what exactly does he say about me. I've bought the house here, sixty-seven thousand, I'm up to my ass in debt, and four kids to be put through college."

"Why the hell don't you talk to Timmons?" Oliver asked in quiet anger.

"Because I'd be admitting I'm scared. I don't mind admitting it to you. Sure, I take a drink now and then. You understand. You're good about it, taking over, getting me home, pouring me in the door to my beloved wife."

Rain slammed the car and Oliver thought about the gun locked away several feet from him. Self-preservation was always a good idea. He skillfully mixed truth with falsehood.

"I've lost count of how many envelopes he's given me. I opened one and it was just blank paper. If you'll start the car and get us out of this Gomorrhha . . ." watching the sea gone white, gone wild, in another blaze of lavender, "I'll skim through the others and see if you're among those present. And if so I'll black you out. Thoroughly."

"And you'll let me know, one way or another, later tonight? Say I call you about ten." Lamb began backing the car out of the dunes.

"All right." Oliver suddenly felt invaded, used, enraged. Dragged into office spites and pettinesses, pulled down onto the antheap with the rest of them. His gratifications in life were not centered in his work; his work merely paid for them, set the important part of him free. Now here he was mired in miniature intrigue, set about with gnats that might after all turn out to have poison in their tiny stings.

"Step One taken care of," Lamb said. Oliver supposed Timmons was Step Two but profoundly wasn't interested.

"One thing," he said. "Once is too often to do anything to me, too. You might pass it around in the men's room—while they're nailing up the no-smoking sign—that I've put Timmons' report cards in a safe deposit box at my bank."

Running up the front steps, out of the rain, he had never found 222 more pleasant to come home to. The high-ceilinged white-painted ample rooms welcomed him. He made himself a martini, took two lamb chops and a fat Jersey tomato out of the refrigerator, put a potato in to bake, and got the batch of envelopes out of his shirt drawer. They were numbered. He opened Number 1 with no attempt to conceal the signs of the swift impatient tearing.

Lamb wasn't hard to find.

(Item #5. John Lamb, a senior chemist in R and D, is often intoxicated in the afternoons, and therefore probably incapable of productive work. He . . .

He stopped reading. In savage disgust, he got a felt-tipped pen and crossed out Lamb and everything about him.

He had no intention of going to the ludicrous lengths of hiring a safe deposit box. But, just in case some other idiot might come looking for the envelopes—perhaps at a time when he was away, and Lou, unsuspecting kind Lou, was here alone—he'd better secure them, away from the white clapboard house.

Lamb called him at ten o'clock. Oliver had done some reluctant final pondering. Say he wasn't mentioned? New envelopes (although he was going to cut *them* off) and more going-home back-road questioning. Tell the whole truth, and put poor kicked, malice-steaming Timmons on the spot?

He said, disliking every word, "Nothing to worry about, John. Just some blathering about your having taken two and a quarter hours for lunch some day in May. And using language he thinks is unsuitable in front of the secretaries. You're in between the watery mashed potatoes in the cafeteria"—of which there was no mention—"and the day they ran out of paper towels in the men's room"—another invention.

"You're not being, just, tactful, are you?" Lamb asked.

Oliver fought to keep the boredom out of his voice. "No. And it's crossed out anyway. While we're on the subject, I hope and assume you won't tell anyone about your recent buccaneering. I don't want other people flourishing deadly weapons in my face."

"Of course not," Lamb said heartily. "And I know you, from what they say about you. Silent as the grave. Thanks a lot, Oliver."

At 8:30, twenty minutes before Lamb would pick him up, Oliver wrapped Timmons' envelopes in waterproof clear plastic. He strolled up the block under the weeping Norway spruces, past a noble tulip tree, to the yellow-painted house with a For Rent sign on the lawn. He had noticed before that the wood latticing was loose on one side of the porch.

He pulled it aside, watched by a bluejay on a nearby branch, lay down and got into the crawl-space under the porch, and taped the package to the dry sound boards two feet over his head. A *very* safe deposit box. And sorry, Timmons, but screw you, now and indefinitely.

He got to his feet, replaced the lattice panel, and dusted the spruce needles off his seersucker trousers. He looked at the splendid bluejay and addressed him merrily.

"And that," he said, "is the end of that."

EIGHT

Lou had climbed to her high attic to put away, finally, in July, the winter clothes she wore down here. All right, Mr. Decimus Finch, you get all my efficiency and there's none left over for me.

She went to the window to look at the tulip tree in the shining morning and observed Oliver's lithe mysterious wriggle out from under the porch of the yellow house. Rescuing a bird or a kitten maybe, but if so there was no sign of the rescued in his immediate vicinity.

Yes, mysterious, but interestingly so. Of course, he didn't know she was here, on a Friday morning. She had gotten Decimus Finch off to a conference in London and had decided to treat herself to a long weekend. Driving down late Thursday, she had left her ailing car at the garage near the bus station and walked the quiet fragrant mile home. You could still walk, alone, in the dark in Farms River, without a qualm.

Maybe today, she thought, amused and annoyed at her single-track mental process, I'll run across that girl of his.

She went unhurriedly down the two flights of stairs and on through to her bedroom at the front of the house, to make her bed. Oliver was sitting on the steps reading the New York *Times*, waiting for his ride.

He wore a fresh gray-and-white striped suit and a pale yellow shirt. Little as he seemed to go out, at least on weekends, he had somewhere acquired the kind of apricot tan she associated with delightful tow-headed sand-castling little boys on her early childhood beaches.

Over the top of the white cafe curtain, she said, "Hello, Oliver."

"Lou!" He looked surprised, and pleased. "But your car's not here–?"

"I didn't sneak down on you, honest, to see if you were given to throwing hash parties on the front lawn," Lou said. "I had to leave my car at the garage last night."

"Too bad, I was going to carry you off to swim tomorrow, early, if I could have persuaded you out of bed."

"I think you could have." Now it was she who was surprised and pleased, very.

Lamb's car drew up at the foot of the herringbone brick walk, and he waved her good-bye with his *Times* and got into it.

From the very first weekend, she had decided that the best strategy would be no strategy at all. She was convinced that he would see through even the subtlest tactics.

He had signed a two-year lease; this gave her a nice sense of all-in-good-time. If you can't make it in two *years,* Lou, throw in the towel; although she had always been a right-away kind of girl in her deepest feelings about people, and she suspected that he was by nature as instinctively responsive.

The second weekend, to put him thoroughly at his ease in sharing a house with an unattached young woman, she had invited Tommy Larkin down. They had a comfortable undemanding enjoyment in each other. He was an art director at Y and R. They were eating lunch on the front steps–a nice new Oliver habit–when there was the sound of descending footsteps and Oliver came out through his doorway onto the porch. Introductions were made; Oliver asked Lou if he could borrow her bicycle for half an hour and then disappeared around the side of the house.

"He paints," Tommy Larkin said.

"How do you know?"

"Couldn't you smell the turpentine when he opened the

door? And there's raw umber under his thumbnail, otherwise his hands are respectably tidy."

So that was the nice, clean, unfamiliar odor that sometimes leaked through from his stairwell into her bedroom.

Tommy looked at her thoughtfully. "Married? Or is he alone here?"

"Alone, at least last weekend . . ."

"Queer?"

"I don't think so, do you?"

"No," Tommy said. "Mind your manners in his direction, Lou. Unlimited opportunities for carrying on, just the two of you here."

There were unlimited opportunities, but Oliver seized none of them. He was pleasant, amiable, friendly and calmly charming without any effort at all.

Weekends when she hadn't guests there, they began their sharing of Saturday drinks, providing the gin turn and turn about. Once she had asked him, very casually, if he'd like dinner, she had a small cold roast chicken, and he had declined with thanks and said he had to get back to work, the weekends were no sooner started for him than they were over.

Shyly, she had said, "You paint . . . ?"

"Yes, how did you know?" He looked startled. Did he suspect her of secret prowling around his premises, when he was away from 222?

"Once in a while, the smell of turpentine . . ."

"Oh God, is it reeking all over your house? I'm sorry."

"No, I like it. Clean. A little like lilacs."

"I *told* your renting agent," Oliver said, "that you must be a good-natured girl. And soon I'll show you a painting or two, if you'd like. It's just that I didn't want to bore you."

One Saturday an old olive-green MG in lovingly-cared-for condition stopped at the brick walk. Lou had striped her hair deliberately unevenly with peroxide and was giving it twenty minutes in the sun.

A girl got out of the car, small, slender, tossed short red hair, creamy skin, comically sunburned nose. Halston trousers suit, water-green and loose-legged, five hundred dollars. She stood in the middle of the walk and called, to the upstairs windows, "Oliver!"

Lou couldn't see his head emerge, around the angle of the house wall, but she heard him.

"Go away and come again another day," he said, half laughing.

"I won't. I've come to hijack you. A beach morning, it's a perfectly beautiful day. I have chilled avocados, and peaches, and rolled-up chicken and watercress sandwiches, and four icy icy martinis in the thermos."

"Oh, all right," Oliver said. "All *right*, Polly. Give me five minutes . . ."

"I won't, you might cut and run out the back door, but then you don't have one, do you. I'll come up and help you change."

She gave Lou in her lounge chair an assessing look, ducked her head in a casual hello, and ran up the porch steps into the house.

It rained greenly, heavily, all the following weekend. They had their drinks in Lou's quarters. "Martinis tonight, cozier, I think, in the deluge," Oliver said.

She was standing at the counter trying to get the cap off a bottle of olives; the bottle was taken from her hand and the top removed. He was shoulder-to-shoulder with her as he got the ice-cube tray out and gave the handle a hearty yank.

He looked for a moment at the loosened cubes. "Glasses in the cupboard right over your head," she said, but he didn't seem to hear her. He turned and looked into her eyes. His face was not a foot away from hers.

She knew with her mind and body that he wanted to touch her, perhaps do more than touch her. She watched his eyes haze faintly. She was unable to remove hers from his gaze and found that she had almost stopped breathing.

Rain tapped the panes over the sink and ran jerkily down them in front of the hanging basket outside, blue and white petunias. That was the only sound in the kitchen.

Then he made another sound that was something like a sigh and turned away a little and opened the wall-hung cabinet and got out two cocktail glasses.

As if in partial explanation, he said, "You smell marvelous. And you look . . ." Abruptly, "Where d'you keep your gin?"

Oh, *hell*, she thought. "Pantry there by the door." She looked, how, to him? Clean well-cut white jeans, rose-and-white striped cotton jersey from France. And she'd given her hair a hard swinging brushing, the bangs were getting too long so she had swept them up and off her forehead, which seemed to her an all-right-enough forehead, if a little high, and a little rounded like the rest of her face.

They took their glasses into the sitting-dining room, where there was a deep sofa in the long bay window looking out into the dogwood branches, the ground underneath covered with ivy.

Oliver, drink in hand, prowled, but not restlessly, studying the white brick fireplace, the old panes in the corner cabinet full of delightful odds and ends, cut crystal, blue-and-white ware, her mother's collection of church-fair pitchers, painted candlesticks, old platters standing on edge.

There were great hanging ferns in the bare top halves of the five windows, above the fresh white cafe curtains. A painting over the mantelpiece that held him a moment or two. Three little girls in white, sashed, dimly seen under the immense green cloud of the old lilac on the back lawn. "You, Lou? One of them?" "No, generations ago . . . my father liked it and bought it with the house. It was always there, over the fireplace."

"I love this house of yours," he said. "Downstairs and upstairs. There's something about it . . . I like it as well as any place I've ever lived, or better."

The door to her bedroom was partly open; he looked interestedly in. A lot of blue and white, a big peaceful high room.

No closets, but great tall white-painted wardrobes on either side of the window looking out onto the side porch with its white rail and round sturdy corner pillars.

He came back and sat down on the other end of the squashy flowered sofa.

"It is a nice house," Lou said. "I suppose I don't see it with your fresh eye, we spent summers here when I was a kid and always came down from New York for Thanksgiving and Christmas."

"I thought when I was dragged kicking and screaming to Jersey I'd end up wall-to-walled with a used-car lot across the road and gas stations to the right and left of me. Or mortuaries," he added, thinking of his ride to the sea with Lamb.

An appalling kind of insight hit her. He was looking, not at her, but at the worn but handsome Mahal on the floor, fawn and pale brown, deep blue and faded turquoise and ruddy red.

I love this house . . .

Well, then don't mess things up, getting involved physically or emotionally or both, with your landlady. Sticky. Sloppy. When it's over, when you tire of her or she of you, trouble. Jealousies, recriminations. Tranquility gone. Impossible to stay here, it's not the right atmosphere for painting in peace. Have to be wall-to-walled after all.

He took a thoughtful sip which emptied his glass, and ate his olive. "I have the strangest feeling, Lou, that you're somewhere inside my head."

"I was," she said over her steadily sinking heart. And added, "I was just wondering when you would come to a decision to finish that, and get us another one."

She extended the weekend that began with winter-clothes stashing and Oliver under the porch up the street, through Monday.

In the sunny silent house, on Monday morning, a familiar devil whispered in her ear, tugged at her arm.

She had never been invited upstairs to see his apartment, his atmosphere, the walls that held him. She wondered if her curiosity was neurotic, unnatural; it certainly was immense. But you did feel people in the places they inhabited, feel them close and warm. Like touching a cheek, or stroking a head of slippery dun-colored hair . . .

No. Certainly not. Poking and prying, unforgivable. Especially with someone as private as he was, as contained.

Perhaps, her devil murmured, there won't be another day this whole summer when you're here and he's safely away at work.

Did he return home for his lunch? She doubted it. Anyway, that would probably be between twelve and two. It was eleven o'clock now. Go pick a bowlful of lavender cosmos from the back border. Or, just to keep her wicked self busy, wash the floor-length table cover on the round table in the big kitchen, cornflowers and poppies on now not quite pristine white. Or—

She forgot where she kept the key to the front door, and then remembered. It was in the tiny white willowware pitcher in the corner cabinet.

It's not my devil after all at my heels, she told herself as she went, head up and back straight, around the house. It's that red-headed girl who was going to help him change his clothes. If she keeps things upstairs, well, that's it. Put a crisp end to an infatuation already badly overshadowed if not doomed by plain, simple real estate.

She unlocked the door and went into the small hall and up the pumpkin-painted steps, directly facing the front of the house. The scent, very faint now: turpentine. There was a large open landing on three sides at the top of the stairs. To the right, the small bedroom, which had once been her nursery, and which he had told her he had taken over as his studio. Facing Lambert Road, the great long bedroom, her parents', that was now his living room, and beyond that the large bathroom, much better in every way than the little one she had, installed in a nook of the lower hall when the top floor had been converted into the apartment.

The layout, from childhood, was of course perfectly clear in her mind. But now, it was all, somehow, completely different.

She remembered it as a floor principally for sleeping, for napping. Chintzes and dimities, lazy long-cushioned wicker chairs, big painted bureaus, shades drawn against the hot summer sun.

Brightness around her, uninhibited light. The feel of leisure, laziness, all gone; the silent air seemed to crackle. The apartment was pleasantly underfurnished, airy, looking larger. No connoisseur herself, she recognized what were a few good French and English pieces, walnut, faded mahogany. A stack of art books on the floor beside a comfortable contemporary chair. More books in shelves newly built in between windows. Some kind of Persian scatter rugs she couldn't identify, wonderful blues and bronzes in them. Oblongs of sunlight, striking the painted floors, showed a light film of dust. Casual untidiness here and there, hastily made big bed, knee socks on the little rug beside it, yellow sweater hooked over the top corner of the bedroom door.

Hurry, hurry. She seemed to have some kind of obstruction in her throat. The bedroom closet door was partway open. Nice clothes, men's, nothing female to be seen.

The bathroom smelled of soap and there was a great thick white towel on the floor beside the tub. Not that she was *looking*, but—no make-up, no perfume, on the sleek white counters on either side of the marble sink.

Her nursery, his studio. Canvases leaning against the wall, perhaps a dozen. Another canvas on the big easel, partly finished? although she had no way of telling. Semi-abstract, blurred yet bold, soft but strong, what looked to be dunes and sea and sky in a stormy gray-mauve light, a light so strangely real and enveloping that she was suddenly startled to look beyond it, out the window, into the gold and green of the summer morning. Her fingers itched to go through the others. The outward-facing one was her house, seen under and through the slumber of its trees, again strong, blurred, simplified, as if a near-sighted artist had deliberately taken off his glasses to go to work; the remote peace of the house poured out of the painting.

Better not, don't push your luck. She went back for a moment to the living room to look again at the picture over the French desk but really to—honestly, I'm like a *dog,* she thought—sniff Oliver's air. Faint smell of him, grassy, was it something he wore or did his skin naturally smell that way?

At the foot of the stairs, there was the sound of the door opening, and then feet running up. She froze. Oliver stopped in the doorway of his living room, and stared, his hazel eyes very wide.

"Looking for something?" he asked coldly. "Or just looking."

She was scarlet and stammering. "I'm sorry, but t-there was a—a funny sound in the pipes downstairs, a gurgling, I couldn't find anything down there and I thought—last year there was trouble upstairs with the bathtub pipes—" Even to her, especially to her, it sounded made up on the spur.

"Of course, it's your house." He moved a little into the room and for a moment she was frightened of his calm, feeling the anger under it.

"Too bad I had a dentist's appointment down the street, or you could have had the place to yourself, all day if you wanted. To research the plumbing. By the way, did you track down the trouble?"

She was completely unable to speak and he seemed to take pity on her discomfort. In an altered voice, on the surface pleasant, friendly, he said, "Is it okay with you what I've done in the kitchen? The new cabinets? There weren't any there at all, so—"

"I didn't look in the kitchen," she said wretchedly, and in a last futile attempt to get herself back, "The noise didn't seem to be coming from there."

"Well, then, come look," he said politely. "Not expensive, I'm afraid, but they hold my pots and pans and dishes, and I had to buy this refrigerator, there wasn't one . . ."

"Looks very nice," still wretched. "Sorry that you had to."

"As you see, the breakfast dishes not done yet, I usually do the whole clutter once a day, after dinner." He went on relentlessly, "You probably noticed, in the bathroom, that the floor is my towel rack, as my mother used to say. I pick that up too, at night, to let it dry out."

She drew a deep breath and squared her shoulders. As he hadn't used her name, she wouldn't use his. "Will you please, now, let me out of the principal's office and back to my classroom? I promise never again to cheat on my examination in French."

"I had no idea I was keeping you here," Oliver said.

Quick, down his stairs, but don't scurry. Not like a dog, now; down, and out his door, like a scalded cat.

NINE

Lamb obediently passed along his information, in the 4G men's room at the time of maximum traffic, after lunch, to Joe Beadon, who sat in the pool just behind Ralph Horner.

Not a subtle man, but experienced in the ways of office deceit and knowing a near-truth was better than a fabrication, he said without troubling to lower his voice:

"That nutty bastard Timmons—no, no, don't worry, he was coming out as I was coming in. Well, anyway, I asked Oliver Lee, kidding, you know, whether I'd made the list. He said he didn't know and hadn't looked. Now me, I'd gobble those envelopes up. But he just files them away in a safe deposit box at his bank. Funny kind of guy, when you think of it."

"Are you sure?" Beadon asked. "About the box, I mean. He could just say that, to keep people off his back, maybe going through his desk or wherever he lives . . ." He was leaning against a sink, cleaning his nails.

Lamb gave him a troubled look. "But he *said* so."

"My grandmother used to tell me, People say more than their prayers. If I was him I'd just throw the whole bundle into Farms River, along with the beer cans and junk from the boats. Safer."

It rapidly wove itself into the skein of office gossip.

"Finstal is out sick, he's in the hospital, back trouble was his story but I heard hemorrhoids."

"If it was anyone but Finstal I'd be sorry for him . . . Did you hear Oliver's taken a *safe* deposit box to put Timmons' envelopes in? Well, maybe not taken one, maybe had one already, but anyway he puts them there. At his *bank*."

"Maybe there's something in that crazy list after all, Oliver's a real cool guy . . . what d'you suppose they'll actually do about it, whoever Les mails it to?"

"Don't let me forget to tell you what someone told me about Marie Eggena . . . but, about the list, they'll either think he's off his rocker, and maybe say get rid of him, or—I don't know, there was some trouble in Dallas, somebody stealing inside stuff and selling it to some other company, and they sent a security detective or something from the Swiss office . . ."

"My girl friend was transferred out there, now you mention it. She said it was rough, all kinds of people including her hauled in for questioning, like with the Nazis or something. What about Eggena?"

"Having drinks with Ives, late, after eleven, at the Captain's Deck at Point Pleasant. I didn't see them, but Bess did."

"Well, do you think she got that job because of her *brains?* Can't you just hear him on the phone to his wife? I'm working late, dear, don't wait up."

"While we're on the subject, watch out for that letch Baker. He managed to bump into me near the water fountain, and then he asked me if I was wearing a bra. I mean, the nerve."

"And Veronica says Timmons is writing an engraved invitation to get himself canned."

"Canned or" giggle, "murdered stone cold dead. Veronica's a card, isn't she?"

"But you know, I wouldn't like to be sitting right in front of him. Talking, and kidding, during the day. I mean, from a distance, who'd know what Timmons was talking to her *about?*"

"Morning, Oliver," Kalish said, gliding in and closing the door behind him. He stood over the drawing board, hands in his pockets.

The summer sun did nothing kindly to his sallow skin, but had turned it a bitter greenish-brown. The color, and the small dark watchful eyes, gave Oliver a faint impression of a lizard, waiting flicker-tongued on his rock.

He was working on the design for a box to contain a new eye cosmetic product, Flutterlids. The box was in the shape of a butterfly. There was a piece of rough copy from Thompson, on which the copywriter had scrawled, "Ask that divine Oliver what he can do with this. I don't know where to go from 'flutter.' Japanese fans maybe? Except we don't want to crisscross with those Japanese cosmetics."

When the box lid was lifted, delicate little pots identically matched the ovals and rounds of color on the butterfly's black-edged markings.

Kalish began, "I can see you're busy, dear boy—"

"I'm nobody's dear boy except my mother's," Oliver said.

Taking this as repartee, Kalish grinned whitely. "About this project of poor Timmons . . ."

"The only thing I know about it is that I don't want to know anything about it at all. Or hear anything."

"My point is, as he seems to trust you . . . after all, he's well over the hill, he's bought a house here, the job market in New Jersey is depressed to put it mildly . . ."

"Are you saying you're going to fire him? Unless he ceases and desists?"

"No. If we got rid of all the demi-crazies," confidential and contemptuous, "the place would be only half-staffed." He found himself wanting to amuse Oliver, get over the barrier of distaste he felt coming from the other man. "You know Florrie Vetch in Accounting and Billing? She carries all her valuables, fake jewelry, a prehistoric mink scarf and God knows what else, in two tatty shopping bags that she brings to work with her every *day*. In case her house is robbed."

"It takes all kinds," Oliver said, deliberately offering the uninterested platitude.

"But Timmons—the head office is bound to think he's demented. Then there'd be nothing we could do to stop them. Over and out." He added, "There was an angry man in their plant in Brazil, nothing more than some kind of clerk person, who once set fire to the research laboratories."

"Anger thereafter disallowed at Bela," Oliver said with a

cool agreeing nod of the head, while he laid in, with his brush, a silvered violet circle on one of his butterfly's wings.

Bitch, Kalish thought, fascinated. But, from what he knew of him, a no go.

Oliver rinsed his brush in water. "Why don't you talk to Timmons yourself, as I seem to keep asking."

"I had occasion recently to refuse him a raise, so he probably hates my guts—pity the poor personnel man. I'd only goad him onward and upward."

Oliver considered it odd that a man in his job would be so indiscreet, indecent almost, in his disclosures. Was he worried on his own behalf?

Some homosexual slip of his on the list? Not having anything to do with morals—who gave a corporate damn about morals? But an expense or disfavor of some kind to the company?

Kalish was uncomfortable under the lifted thoughtful gaze.

"Look," he said, "a word from you might save the poor bastard's whole future. That's all I came to say."

Oliver omitted to comment that Kalish looked to be the last person in the world to care about the poor bastard's future.

"I'll think about it," he said. And looked with great attention at his watch.

Kalish, accustomed to dismissing others, was dismissed.

People looking away from people. Stepping over bodies on subway steps. I didn't want to touch him, I thought he might wake up and hit me, officer, or mug me. The classic Genovese case, people watching while a woman was killed under their noses. I don't want to get involved. I have my own life to live.

And what a *bore* all this was.

A man has a right to his fancies. Everybody has to have some kind of escape hatch. This is Timmons' time in the sun, he feels fresh and powerful, he thinks there's at last a good reason for getting up in the morning and shaving and showering and putting on his clothes and coming in to the office which has used him, and misused him, their odds-and-ends man . . .

A word from you might save his whole future.

Oliver sighed. "Oh, shit," he murmured in the direction of his pencil sharpener.

Veronica heard him and laughed. "From the elegant Mr. *Lee?* But you pronounce it better than anybody."

At the end of the day, he said to Timmons, "If you'll drop me off home afterward, I'll buy you a drink on the way."

Timmons' look of radiance gave him an uneasy feeling; he had looked that way all afternoon.

"I'd like that, Oliver. Sort of a celebration," he added in a whisper.

Oliver's heart sank a little. Too late, probably. The deed done? Or maybe the thing completed, ready to be sent.

Timmons took a lusty gulp of his manhattan and fell to coughing. "Too strong," he said, "but according to you that's what drinking is all about. I forgot to say cheers." His eyes were streaming water.

"Les, none of my business, but I think you should think twice, and hard, before you take the pin out of your hand grenade and heave it. Have you thought what might happen to your job? This is a hell of a time to be looking for work."

"Thanks, Oliver—for worrying, I mean. It's very kind of you, but—" The lighted-up look again. "I mailed it this noon. Registered, airmail. It cost a small fortune."

He'd gotten up to Item #50 two weeks ago, but he waited for Lara's semi-annual week's visit to her mother in Media, Pennsylvania. She left on Saturday, and he spent most of the rest of the weekend doing the finished typing. Each page had to be perfect; there could be no appearance of erasures, x'ings out, of fumbling uncertainty and mind changing. A backaching, eye-straining job, and not on the big sumptuous electric he was used to at work, but an old manual. Fresh ribbon, though, crisp white bond paper. If he said so himself, it looked impressive. Authoritative.

He made his covering letter brief and brisk. Mustn't sound peevish, complaining, long-winded. Mustn't come over as some kind of crank. Just an introduction to the hard facts which were to follow.

Walking out of the Goodwood post office that hot gray noon, he felt a sense of elation, of triumph, he had never before in his life known. By God, he thought, Lester will treat Timmons to something special, and right now.

He went into a bar called the Welcome-U and to the bartender's astonishment—after clearing his throat and adjusting his gold-rimmed glasses—ordered a split of champagne. "Best you've got." He sipped it, high on his crest of joy, relishing the cold crispness, the way the bubbles tickled his palate. Better eat soon, he was feeling so delightful that he was almost feeling unreal.

After the last drop of his champagne was savored, he ordered the special, frankfurters and baked beans, roll and butter, ice cream and coffee, $1.50, and consumed it all.

He still felt a little airborne when he went back to his car. So, if I'm a little drunk, so what? he thought blithely. Look at Lamb. Item #6. Nothing very burdensome to do this afternoon, just a page or so of the *Bela Beacon,* and he had squirreled away some material, the new Bela Big Brothers Club, Brent's speech to the Kiwanis (now that he thought about it, that alone would fill two pages) and Rosalie's engagement to a young man in Hair Products.

Looking up as he got into his car, he saw a high white jet trail. By tomorrow, probably, his letter would be up there, 35,000 feet up, winging its way to Geneva. He saw efficient secretarial hands slitting open the long, heavy envelope, eyes glancing to see if it deserved the attention of Marcus Bela, grandson of the founder, and chairman of the board. A gasp, a scurry of feet. "I hate to bother you, Monsieur Bela, but—*it is vital that you look at this document immediately*" . . .

Veronica finished writing a leaflet on a new indigestion remedy tentatively named Indigex. She had been typing hard for an hour and a half and now allowed herself to relax a little.

Yawning, stretching, she turned around to Timmons and asked him for a cigarette. "Write enough about sour stomach and before you know it you've got one," she said. "Or maybe it was that jelly doughnut this morning. It tasted like last week's grease. What are you looking so pleased about, Les?"

For some reason he wanted to keep it to himself, hug it to himself, for a day or so, the thrilling trip to the post office, the moment of mailing, the envelope leaving his hands, passing across the counter. No more, the familiar crackling of the papers in his breast pocket when he put on his suit coat.

Let some people worry, wonder, a few more days, it was nice to get the wary glances, to hear little silences fall when he passed by knots of people, talking and drinking coffee. Underneath his glow there was the most peculiar sense of loss, of something stopped, over–

But that was silly, this was just the very beginning of the real drama. One shoe had been dropped. All he had to do was wait for the resounding crash of the next one.

Yes, keep them guessing. Watching him. Talking about him to each other, maybe even having bad dreams about him.

Looking up from his account of Rosalie's engagement, he said, "Wouldn't *you* be pleased if you had only six inches to go on the bottom of the last page of the *Bela Beacon*?"

In the ladies' room, "Take it from me," Veronica said to Bess Murphy, "he's mailed it off. Right straight to Switzerland. I know him. He's never looked this way before, I mean, never. Like a cat who ate a whole *flock* of canaries and just isn't hungry any more."

For political and community relations reasons, Bela kept fat balances in the Goodwood National, Farms River First, and Lakewood Citizens' banks; in all three, they were by far the largest depositor.

Augusta Lansing, a new teller, took the call when the manager was out getting his ten o'clock container of coffee from the drugstore across the street.

"I'm calling for Mr. Lee, at Bela," the voice said, a man's. Augusta snapped to attention at the magic name. "He's away and he asked that some papers be put in his safe deposit box. He *does* have a box with you . . . ?"

"I'll check, just a moment—" And then, "No, sorry, sir, but he does *bank* here." She had seen him twice and remembered his face with pleasure.

"That's against the rules, Augusta," her neighboring teller said. "Talking about boxes. Don't let *him* know. And me, I never heard you."

TEN

Oliver as a rule avoided parties, finding that the good gathering together was heavily outnumbered by the boring and bad. But he hadn't quite been able to get out of this one. He'd bumped into McGinnis in the fish store. McGinnis had been fired when Bela moved down from New York. He had sat in the next office to Oliver and by coincidence lived in the same brownstone on West Twelfth Street in the Village.

They had been associates, not particularly friends, but McGinnis fell on him like a long-lost brother. It turned out that he had gotten a job with Mycroft, a great job, he said, three thousand greater than the one he'd lost. And bought a great new house, and the kids loved living near the shore, and Madge had already made a pile of friends. Oliver must, man, come to their little Saturday night bash. The invitation was from two weeks back.

Regretting saying yes, he had considered taking Polly, whom he thought of, now a little doubtfully as his, more or less, girl; very attractive but she got in the way of his work, and occasionally she talked too much. A bad sign. People needed silences to feed on. And besides—she was spending this weekend in East Hampton, having unsuccessfully tried to get him to go with her.

His taxi dropped him there at 7:30, a journey of less than two miles. It was as bad as he had feared, or a little worse. Thirty or forty cars for the little bash, parked for a block around the no doubt overpriced ranchhouse, new, brick, on its trim shrubberied corner lot. Kids by the dozens out in back uproariously barbecuing, supervised by a sullen-faced

McGinnis son of nineteen or so. Inside, suburban strangers, the futility of introductions to people whose names he couldn't remember and whom he would never see again.

The women, mostly, in the living room. The price of food. Have you found a good doctor, Madge? See that nice girl beside the piano—may I call you Oliver? Don't you think she's pretty? She's just been divorced.

The men in the kitchen, the dirty stories that had been fresher and funnier in New York, the same stories, a year to three years ago. "Let me fill you up again, Oliver, and there's a ton of food on the dining-room buffet but hell, it might be more fun when you get hungry to go out back where the action is, with the kids, and have them grill you a dog or a burger . . ."

"You're not leaving *already*, Oliver?" "Sorry, I have a friend coming down for the rest of the weekend, and he's probably sitting on my steps waiting to get in right now." "*He?*" Well-scotched arch giggle. "Who're you kidding, Oliver?"

He had politely stretched his departure time to after nine o'clock, and he decided to walk home, to clear his head of the smoke and the boredom. When he reached Lambert Road it was very dark, under a heavy cloud cover, the street lights sparingly placed, but his feet confidently knew the sidewalk, heaved slanting by tree roots.

Two odd things, the door was unlocked and when he flicked the light switch in the hall nothing happened. Well, electric light bulbs did blow, with annoying regularity; and on several occasions he had neglected to engage the lock when leaving.

He stood still at the foot of the stairs and found himself listening intently.

Silence, but possibly the wrong kind of silence, someone else, keeping still? His tendrils were out, and they seemed to be trying to tell him something. Lou, pursuing her secret investigations? In the *dark?* Unless, maybe, trouble with the fuses, he had no idea where the fuse box was.

"Lou?" he called, and felt so foolish when there was no answer that he ran lightly and quickly up the steps, and stood and listened a second or two on the landing. There was a little round table to his right, with a lamp on it. He thumbed the switch. Again, nothing. Of course, the fuses. Life in the country, rough and ready. There had been a storm last night, maybe it had blown the whole works out.

Lou, in case this ever happened, and she said it did at least once a summer, had given him emergency candles which he had put in the empty bottom drawer of his bureau. He bent to pull the drawer open, heard the swift movement over the drawer noise and almost simultaneously was struck hard over the back of the head.

His forehead smacked the bureau and he sprawled sideways, was clumsily half-lifted, and thrust a few feet forward. A final shove, a muffling of something about his face and chest and shoulders, the slam of a door, the sound of a key being turned in a lock.

He found himself down on one knee. He was partially dazed and for a moment without orientation. It was like getting up from a deep sleep, in the dark, in a strange room, and having no idea where you were. Then he got to his feet in a thicket of trouser legs. He was locked in his own clothes closet, to the left of the bureau.

At first his imprisonment seemed so ridiculous, comical in a way, that he was relieved. Thank God he had four left of his daily ration of six cigarettes. He lit one. Careful, don't burn the pants in your face with the match, that's a new suit.

But what was there to be relieved about? Whoever had locked the door could unlock it and get at the sitting, or rather the wobbly-legged, standing duck inside. And do what to him, more or less defenseless in here? He wanted to shout, but didn't. Safer to be considered still out cold.

He put a tentative shoulder to the paneled wood of the closet door and quietly pushed. Solid as a rock, like everything else in this house. God, would there be *air* . . . ?

Yes, a little. There was a crack of light under the door. The fuses hadn't blown after all. Whoever was out there must have gone around patiently unscrewing light bulbs.

He heard drawers being opened, the bureau, the little desk, long silences between opening and closing noises. The interrupted burglar, or searcher, was at work again, and taking his time about it.

The crack of light disappeared. He thought he heard or sensed feet going down the stairs and the front door closing, but his head was throbbing and his ears rang, these damned clothes. He shoved them to his right and left, along the pole, away from his head.

He was subject to mild claustrophobia; jammed elevators making numerous stops, and small head-touching enclosed spaces bothered him a little.

But don't, no don't, think about the closet and being in it for more than a short time.

Lou's apartment had been dark, but that didn't necessarily mean she hadn't come down. Out being dined, wined, or being made love to, perhaps . . .

He had spent the day in New York, lunching with his sister-in-law, of whom he was fond, and doing galleries morning and afternoon until bus time.

Dismiss the impossible thought of no Lou. She might be downstairs right now, reading, on her sofa. Cheerfully, he began to shout, "Lou. *Lou!*" Deafening in his own ears, but would it penetrate as more than a casual faraway sound through the thick walls?

What if, as sometime in mid-June, she skipped the week-end? She might be harking back to their exchange in the living room here, when he had caught her prowling. He had been, he remembered, not nice to her at all. Poor Lou, blushing about her pipes and her plumbing—

His body, feeling the beginnings of obscure terror before it got to his mind, flung a shoulder once, twice, three times against the door with all the force at its command. The only result was pain, and the sound and feeling of himself as some large lashing trapped animal.

He tried to think about the huge free-moving unaccountable world outside the closet.

Small-time raiders, looking for a television set, a camera, a pair of gold cufflinks? Experienced lock-handlers . . .

Or, had someone gotten hold of his key? Veronica: "Honest to God, Oliver, leaving your jacket on your chair while you come and go . . . I hope you don't keep anything valuable in it." He kept his house key in his change pocket. So easy, to pluck it out, drive to Woolworth's in Goodwood, have it copied, drop it back into the pocket. Any day. Yesterday, or a week back.

Inevitably, infuriatingly, Timmons' fifty gnats, alerted, came flying about in the closet. Lamb, the first gnat. Maybe tonight's visitor Item # what? Unless it was still Lamb, unconvinced. That left either forty-eight or forty-nine attacks to go.

Knowing he was growing badly lightheaded—one was not liable to attack from watery mashed potatoes, if the potatoes weren't, as Lou suggested, an attempt to mislead—he lit his third cigarette. Only one left.

Probably fevered nonsense anyway, connecting this with Timmons' rantings. Look at the little frightened surrounding world, wherever you happened to live, locks and bolts and padlocks, German shepherds, expensive electronic security devices. Honestly, we never go out after dark any more, we're afraid to.

Speaking of dogs, it was time to howl for help again, no matter what his throat felt like. He knew that in the house halfway up the block, just before the yellow house for rent, an old deaf woman lived, but she might have a visitor with ears—

To the right of 222, there was a large old red-and-white wooden summer mansion now taken over by a firm of lawyers, closed and empty at night, especially empty on summer weekends. Nothing across the street but woods, three or four lots in length, too expensive apparently to have been picked up so far.

He had nothing on him, nothing in the closet, that would serve as a tool for an attempt, no doubt futile in any case, at unscrewing the door hinges.

"Lou!" he shouted again, and then caught his breath, got out his handkerchief and wiped his wet face. The bedroom windows were open. Occasional cars would be going by, up and down Lambert Road.

Space it, put your lungs into it. He cried *"Help!"* twenty times. And thought that engine noises would probably, to the drivers, blot him out.

Cool it, calm it. The closet was echoing with him now, raw echoes. Recklessly, he lit the last cigarette and stared at the chalk stripes on a dark gray sleeve, in the brief flare of the match.

Not the whole weekend, here, never the whole . . . weekend.

But what was he thinking about, "weekend"? After that, Monday, Tuesday, Wednesday. He seemed to hear the sound of an unanswered telephone, his, that never stopped ringing. He had no idea how long you could live without food or water, given a reasonably healthy body, but the question was, how long did you stay sane?

Something happening in his head which had nothing to do with the pain, better sit down. The closet was six feet long; he could even lie down, although his sandals and shoes didn't make much of a mattress. But don't go to sleep, the air might stop.

Was that why he was gasping, almost sobbing? Was the air stopping, not enough for this black rectangular space, or for the lungs gulping at it?

Like most people who have managed to survive to adulthood, he had had his share of near misses. An almost fatal automobile accident, but he'd been thrown free of the convertible. A time at thirteen when he'd swum out too far off Montauk and been caught in a rip tide and was, just barely, saved by a lifeguard. A fall from a tall tree when he was very young, four or five.

But this was the worst, the very worst, because then you only worried about your body, your bones and flesh and blood, and you didn't have much time to dwell on that either because it had all happened so fast.

Now you worried about the mind that was locked in the closet. Maybe a day, two days . . . maybe to die, the mind, to die there for good.

In a fashion she described to herself as either cowardly or bridling or both, Lou decided to forgo Farms River this last weekend in July. There was the new Gauguin show at the Museum of Modern Art, and Tommy Larkin wanted her to go with him to a terrace cocktail party thirty stories above the East River, on Sunday.

I mean, I really fixed us, she thought, whatever there is of us. I can see myself waiting, around five, for our drinks together, and no Oliver. Take that, you interfering bitch.

In the end, she split the difference. The weather report for Sunday was alarming. It would be ten degrees cooler down there, and the Andersons, too, wanted her for a pool party Sunday afternoon, under their trees. When you tired of the pool, you could walk across a sandy road and onto the beach and into the Atlantic. And ride the beautiful waves controlled in their violence by the unshelving flat sand below, and soak your face in green and white foam, soak away the blinding oyster-skied week in New York.

She got out her car from the garage in the basement of her apartment building and drove to Farms River. She arrived in the solemn silence of one o'clock in the morning.

The living room smelled of last week's roses, the blue bowl still dropping petals on the coffee table. She opened a few windows, picked up a book that she'd probably be too tired to read very long, and then went yawning into her bedroom and turned back the bed.

It was then she heard the stamping and thumping noises

from above, in a way terrifying noises. What on earth could he be up to, or could *they* be up to? Dancing a polka? There wasn't any music, though.

The thinly carried whisper of a cry, "*Lou*," and, "*Help . . .*"

She got the key again from the little blue-and-white pitcher and ran around the house and up the stairs. The thumping and crying out had stopped and the silence somehow suggested despair.

"Oliver?" She had run distractedly into his living room, found the lights wouldn't go on, groped her way back to the landing, heard something in the bedroom, and located the sound. She wrenched at the knob of the closet door, then her hand dropped to the lock and found the key in it.

He almost fell on her as he plunged wildly out. She swayed aside and he went down on his knees. He was making a strange half-weeping noise in his throat. She reached down a hand to help him, and he said in a torn voice that was painful to listen to, "No, first—screw the light bulb."

She thought he was uttering hysterical imprecations on G.E. bulbs, but he said, "Light, Lou, for Christ's sake *light*," and she gave the bulb a twist to the right and flicked the switch, and looked at what the light showed her, and looked away.

The terror was still there in the staring eyes, the pupils enormous, just thinly rimmed with hazel. He was an awful color under what had been his apricot tan. His exhausted heavy breathing, gasping almost, seemed to fill the room. And his face, his contained face, a tortured gargoyle underlit with the bad green—

"I thought I might be here until next Wednesday," he said. "If I lasted till next Wednesday." His features were dimly clearing. He made an effort to get up and, strong herself, she reached down and half-lifted him and helped him over to the bed and onto it.

"Thieves, someone . . . I don't know," he said, alarming her further by his vagueness. "The lights wouldn't work and I was looking for your candles in that bottom drawer and whoever it was banged me over the head and bundled me into the closet like last week's laundry. And I thought . . ."

He can't put into words what he thought, Lou immediately knew. And no wonder.

Her Decimus Finch efficiency took over. "Stop talking, your poor voice, you're out of it now, everything's all right, Oliver. Have you any brandy here? If not, I have some . . ."

He raised a protesting hand. "Don't go away, don't go away for a few minutes . . . but, whiskey, you need it too . . ."

At maximum speed, she poured two stiff drinks and gave him his with her own now shaking hand. He took a gulp, put the glass down, and reached for the shaking hand and held it against his cheek as though desperate for warmth, contact with another human being, now that he was no longer alone in the world. His own hand was damp and cold. There was a spill of moisture on the side of his nose. Sweat? Tears?

"I have a book downstairs," Lou said softly, as to a child in distress. "We'll have our drink, and then I'll run down and get it, and while I do you take your clothes off and get into bed, underneath the covers I mean, you're shivering. Then I'll make you some hot tea in your kitchen. Then I'll sit in this chair and read, if the light won't bother you . . ."

He turned his head to her and smiled faintly. "The light? You're kidding. It was as dark in there, forever, sort of, as six feet under, Lou . . ."

"That bang on your head . . . I don't see any blood."

He touched the bone behind his ear. His hair looked as though someone had taken an eggbeater to it. "No, just a lump, sore though." Almost in embarrassment, he added, "If I could have gotten a *run* at that door, I might have . . ."

"It's all over and done with, what you need is a good night's sleep. No point in calling the police now, you're in no shape to talk to them and anyone living around here who might have seen the wrong car in front of the house is asleep too. The morning's time enough."

She noticed that while his trembling had stopped an occasional spasm took him from head to foot. He rolled his eyes at her like a nervous horse when she finished her drink and got up.

"Two minutes or less, Oliver." Actually, she allowed him a tactful eight minutes for bed-going. With her book, she brought back a billowy white taffeta comforter and put it over him. His clothes were thrown over the other chair; he had the sheet pulled up to his ears. "You can toss this back later if it gets too hot, but you need it now."

"I can't wreck *your* night like this, Lou," he said, looking up into her face from under his lashes. "Or can I?"

"You're not wrecking it. I'll read here till you convince me you're asleep, and then I'll go and make up the living-room sofa and sleep there, just in case you wake up and want to hear a voice."

"Leave the light on? I've had enough darkness for tonight."

"I will, Oliver."

In a gesture that had nothing erotic about it, she bent and lightly kissed his forehead and smoothed his tumbled hair back.

"Good night, Florence Nightingale." Sighing gone-away voice. In ten minutes, he was asleep.

Once, during the night, she heard a half-strangled cry and got up off the sofa and put her head in at the door. Quiet even breathing; he had made the sound in his sleep.

What if in her peevishness at him—New York or Farms River this weekend—she had decided not to come? Reaction, and delayed wild curiosity about this near-disaster in her house, and thinking what he must have gone through in his clothes closet, kept her awake most of the night.

At seven, after three hours' sleep, sandy-eyed and rumpled in her linen skirt and jacket, she glanced in on him again. He might very well lie there, moons away in time, until twelve. On his kitchen counter, she left a note. "I'll have hot coffee and some breakfast for you whenever you wake up. L."

Going out the front door, she saw a white flickering edge of something on the trunk of the beech tree to the right of the brick walk. She went around the tree to look at the message facing the sidewalk. A sheet of plain white paper, printed with block capitals. "There's a man locked in a closet upstairs at this house. Please let him out or call for help."

What a kindly crook, Lou thought. All he'd do to Oliver was chance his incarceration, alone in the demon-haunted dark, from 9:30 at night to some unspecified hour on the following day. *If* the sign, fastened to the tree bark by a straight pin, hadn't blown away. And *if* anyone paid any attention at all to it.

ELEVEN

Glisteningly shaved and showered, Oliver presented himself at Lou's door a little before noon. He was wearing white drill trousers and a red-and-white gingham shirt and looked entirely himself again.

She went to pour him a cup of coffee. He said, "First things first," and came over and put his arms around her and held her very close, and kissed her slowly and warmly. "Thanks, Lou."

"As they say, I only did what anyone else would do." She hoped he couldn't feel her heart's commotion in her breast.

"As they sing—it ain't what you do it's the way how y'do it," Oliver sang, lightly but suddenly releasing her. Just as I was beginning to get comfortable, she told herself later, deliberately downplaying the embrace, putting it in context. Just natural normal gratitude, directly and sweetly expressed.

She gave him the rescue message from the tree and he studied the printing intently. "Could be anybody," he said. "Some sort of education, though. And a firm hand. Soft-hearted type, but he might have wondered what my first aid would eventually find in the closet. How did he know it was or wasn't air tight? By the way, I'm going to have the locks changed, of course, and do you mind if I have the lock removed from the closet door for the rest of my tenancy here?"

"Need you bother? It's a very simple lock, on the front door, they may have used one of those plastic ruler things."

"Maybe, but just to make sure." He realized now that at the back of his mind, all along, under the panic, he had felt that it was someone from Bela, one of Timmons' Items. The thoroughness of the search eliminated, for him, the possibility of the ordinary fast businesslike snatch of easily salable things. Nothing at all had been missing. His papers in his desk, bills, letters, bank statements, personal documents, had been thrust untidily back in. The bookcase showed that someone had searched behind the books, not troubling to push them tidily back into place. Had, for all he knew, shaken out every single book.

A French porcelain clock worth $500 and two famille vert vases on the mantelpiece had been overlooked, as well as his gold cufflinks and an expensive Swiss watch given him as a present—which he never wore because it kept erratic time.

Looking, then, for three or four long white envelopes.

He thought that the less Lou knew about it, the better; and wished he'd kept his mouth shut to her, about Timmons. Too bad she knew as much as she did about it already.

He finished his coffee. "Now I'm going to go and call the police. Probably useless, but you never know."

He notified the police more as an obligation to his landlady than because of any hope of practical results. After all, it had been her premises that had been broken and entered.

The detective from the Farms River police department arrived half an hour later, dark, young, curly-haired.

It would be nice if the detective, Fraser, would inform him that houses all up and down Lambert Road had been recently rifled. Oliver would much have preferred an ordinary burglar.

"So, nothing missing," Fraser said, after listening with his head cocked. He was writing busily in his notebook. "Breaking and entering, assault and attempted robbery."

"Would you like a beer?"

"If you'll have one—it's a thirsty day out there," Fraser said, grinning happily, and because of the hospitality did a little more delving.

"He was pretty close to you, shoving you around—did it feel like a kid, or what?"

"A kid, or a grown man, or"—Lou's firm strength, lifting

him, helping him, last night—"even a woman, I suppose." He remembered now a strong scent, probably intensified by the heat of fear. "Some kind of perfume, or cologne, but of course all three sexes wear it now."

"Yeah, I do myself. Braggi," Fraser said, supplying the name innocently. "Not on duty, of course. You might recognize it if you smelled it again, but you're not about to go around sniffing everyone in Farms River, I guess?"

"No, and I might smell Braggi on someone, and where would that get me?" He saw no point in offering Fraser the baroque tale of Timmons and his list. The Farms River police were hardly likely to seize the opportunity of interviewing forty or fifty people at a powerful and influential company, over what looked on the books like an aborted everyday robbery.

"Well, okay." Fraser stood up. "Thanks for the beer. It's kind of funny—you say that he came at you from behind?—that he didn't just cut and run down those stairs. But you can't account for what these crazy bastards will do, some of them freaked out of their skulls. I'll ask a few questions around here, see if anyone saw a car, noticed a license number. But the one up the street is deaf and the one across the street from *her* is crazy as they come—but I don't think she's dangerous, hasn't been so far anyway. Take it easy, Mr. Lee."

Must be a little weird himself, he thought, departing. Not even a TV. And no car to steal. Fraser shook his head. Nice guy, though. Good beer, Danish.

He called Oliver forty-five minutes later, from the station. "Nothing. Those two old dolls were asleep, but even if they'd been awake don't hold your breath about what they'd see or remember. Or hear. And you don't get many pedestrians up your way."

Or anywhere, Oliver thought. And returned to the question he had been asking himself, Why me? Why not Timmons?

Once, all right. Lamb had his rider very much at his disposal. Lamb with his wheels and his casually revealed gun. But twice?

Maybe Timmons had, Washington style, leaked to someone

the fact that he had mailed his list. And if you were planning to take any kind of retaliatory action against Timmons, it would be wise to get hold and get rid of the second list, with your name on it loud and clear. Or, a more innocent answer, finding out exactly what you were accused of, to get your own defense ready, your escape hatch open.

Deep, indolent summer afternoon. He flicked his brush, placed a small suggestion of what might be a rowboat in the blue-white dazzle where sea and sky were one. He felt, coming up from below, a sleeping silence about the house. He smiled and lit the third of his six cigarettes, and went to the window to see what was happening in the other world beyond his easel.

A dark blue Rolls-Royce went slowly, inquiringly, past the house. Traffic was busy, people on the way to the beaches; horns signaled the Rolls to pick up its feet. The large majestic car paid no attention, but floated around in a U-turn to the screech of other drivers' brakes and no doubt unheard curses, ambled back along the wooded strip across the road, made another get-out-of-my-way U-turn, and placed itself firmly at the curb, in front of the brick walk.

A man got out, powerful, stocky, middle forties, strong seamed face, white thatch of hair, commanding nose. Well, Spencer Tracy as I live and breathe, Oliver thought. The man marched purposefully up the walk and climbing the porch stairs disappeared from view. The doorbell was imperiously rung.

Oliver opened the door to him.

"I want Ms. Townsend," he was informed, in a voice that was accustomed to get what it wanted.

Oliver returned the other man's head-to-foot survey, and back up again.

"I'm not sure, but I think she's asleep. She only managed a few hours last night, poor girl."

This brought a heavy executive frown.

"It's quite simple, actually, if you know your way around

this house," Oliver added helpfully. "Her door, her front door, is at the back. Through the porch."

"Just exactly who are you?" the man demanded.

"Ms. Townsend's tenant. And you're"—Oliver deliberately omitted the first name—"Finch. Couldn't be anybody else."

Decimus Finch looked as if Spencer Tracy would like to give this young man, this tenant who knew his way about the Townsend house, a good thrashing. Instead, tightening his lips, he turned and strode, yes, strode, Oliver thought, down the steps and to the right.

Ten minutes of sun might be nice. And Lou's bedroom looked out on the porch. He sat down on the top step and prepared shamelessly to listen.

A few seconds later, a light knocking, from the sound of it on the opened bedroom door.

A short silence, and then, drowsily, "Oliver . . . ?"

His name floated out to him seductively, the voice sheeted and pillowed, fresh from the depths of sleep. She must have turned her head and seen Finch in the doorway. "Oh, *Dex* . . ."

"Who the devil is Oliver? Were you by any chance expecting him?"

"As a matter of fact I was dreaming . . . and I never make much sense when I first wake up . . ."

"Is he—is that fellow upstairs here—what's his name? He knew mine but didn't bother to offer his."

"His name is Lee," Lou said, sounding now awake and collected. "And what on earth are you doing here, Dex? Rolls run away with you?"

"Put some clothes on, woman—I can only assume, from here, that you're going to have to start from scratch. I'm a temporary fugitive from a terrible country weekend party in Morristown. Horse people. Dams and sires and grand-dams and grand-sires, enough to drive you up the wall."

"If you'll be kind enough to close the door . . . what time is it?"

"Four-fifteen. Just time to drive you to a place I like on

Long Beach Island and arrive at the crack of cocktail hour. Louise, I've never seen you–mmm–so delightfully tumbled about and inefficient-looking."

Lou's merry, murmuring laugh, deep in her throat. "I *did* ask you to close the door. And as I'm not on duty, how do you know I'm not otherwise occupied this evening?"

"If you're so fixed in our working relationship," Finch said, "I'll dictate a letter to you over your lobster."

No yes-sir, no-sir arrangement; but open, equal. Fond. Well, of course, Oliver found himself thinking, that's my Lou. That's the way she would handle secretarying.

Two of the bedroom windows looked out onto the porch. The shades were pulled halfway down, to the tops of the white cafe curtains. Lou dressing in there now, delightfully tumbled still. Starting from scratch.

He went thoughtfully up his stairs and back to his easel.

Drowsy, dreamer's voice, "Oliver?"

Not fair. He shouldn't have sat on her steps and invaded her waking. "His name is Lee."

He mixed on his palette a glorious orange and joyfully applied it. A bowl of fruit against the summer sea, waiting for the lazy distant swimmers. A fly or two might come in handy. It was almost August, fly time. He did two flickering fruitflies.

Lou came around the house, under his gaze, a limber gardeny girl in something long and soft, flowered and floating. Her hair was caught back with a bow of black-velvet ribbon, the waist-long streamers drifting in the breeze.

Finch, waiting on the lawn, said, "My God, Louise, are we on the way to our wedding?"

"No," Lou said. "Our lobsters and our letter."

Before getting into the Rolls, her eyes flicked instinctively upward and directly into Oliver's.

But how did she . . . ?

He went back to his canvas and painted a plum.

After working all afternoon, he walked a fast two miles to stretch his legs and to try to enlighten his head. During his walk, he found himself wondering, trying to be offhand about it, what was coming next? Bad things being assumed to happen in threes. A Molotov cocktail tossed through his window? A trip wire on the top step of his stairway? No, it wasn't he that they, or he, or she, were after, but the bloody envelopes.

Either Lamb hadn't spread his safe deposit box story widely enough, or somebody hadn't believed it.

He was several blocks from Lambert Road, on his way home, when a car drew up beside him and stopped. Carl Ives got out of it. Dapper, with his small crisp black moustache, his hair cut cautiously long, just nape-covering, his uneasy dark eyes. Pale blue suit a little too glossy, blue tie with a swarm of goldfish on it.

"Afternoon, Oliver. You live down on the far corner, don't you?"

Oliver wanted to say why? But instead said yes.

Timmons, he thought, couldn't possibly have passed up the juicy tale of Marie Eggena's sudden ascendancy to power as Ives' assistant. Was Ives returning to the scene of the closeting to sniff around and find out if there had been an unfortunate final smothering in the white house at the corner of Lambert and Jefferson?

Then, disliking the feeling of becoming obsessed, he made a bland statement on the beauty of the afternoon, and was interrupted by Ives.

"Won't keep you, but can you tell me anything about that yellow house on the corner up from where you live?" Were the dark eyes boring into him, or did Ives always have that intense examining look?

"Tell you what about it?"

"Well, it's for sale—and you living in the neighborhood, you might know if it's a sound house or not. The porch looks a bit saggy. Needless to say the real estate man will swear it's sound as a bell, but the locals usually have the lowdown on houses. I'm in the market, we've been renting at Bayside and it's costing us a fortune. I tried to get a look through the windows, but they're dusty of course . . ."

Oliver had a mental vision of Ives, peering, probing, circling the yellow house. He tried to remember if the car beside them, a dark blue car, had gone by when he had crawled in and then out from under the porch. Cars were things he didn't notice.

It wouldn't have to be the blue car. It could have been anybody's car, anybody at Bela. Over morning coffee– And what do you think Oliver was up to, at eight-thirty this morning?

Oh, for God's sake. He shook his head impatiently as if an insect had lighted upon his hair.

"I don't know a thing about it, not even the price," he said, starting down the sidewalk with a casual backward wave of his hand. "See you."

TWELVE

"What does Timmons do with himself Saturday mornings?" Ralph Horner asked.

"Walks on the boardwalk at Seaside Park, rain or shine," Veronica said. "Two miles at least. Has ever since he moved here, he's always trying to sell me the sea air, but I like to sleep Saturdays . . . anyway, why?"

"My car's out of whack and I thought I might borrow his for an hour or so to pick up some stuff at Sears. I live only about a quarter of a mile away from him. But I guess that's out."

Every house in Golden Valley had what the developers mysteriously called a Bermuda Porch. This was a narrow flagged oblong extending across the house front, roofed, with two spindly 4×4's to support the roof. "The dignity of a pillared facade," said the brochure. Garden furniture could be placed here, a little of it; the streets and lanes and the other houses could be watched at leisure.

What with gardening, gossiping, sunbathing, shouting at noisy children to shut up, and arrivals from and departures to the A&P, the Acme, the ShopRite, the Saturday morning scene was a busy one.

Rod Nevins, a sixteen-year-old boy with a complexion disturbed to what might be looked upon as outright anger, was going slowly by on his bicycle, his pace indicating he was headed nowhere in particular, when the big stout man came down the flagged walk of the Timmons house.

"Hey, kid." He stopped beside a black Mercury parked in front. "What kind of a dirty old man lives there?" He winked.

"Just Mr. Timmons. And Mrs. Timmons." But Rod pricked up his ears. "Dirty how?"

The man gestured to the porch, where there was a large cardboard box. "I just delivered sixty dollars worth of the stuff to him. Porn. I have this store in Goodwood. He stopped in last night with his order, it's all paid for, wanted it this morning."

He took out his wallet. "Hey, for a dollar will you keep your eye on it till he gets home? See nobody steals it?"

"Sure will," Rod said. He waited until the Mercury pulled away and then putting two fingers in his mouth emitted a piercing whistle. The whistle always conveyed to his friend Joe next door, *action*. Joe came running.

The carton was loosely tied, no trouble to untie it. Rod had his story all ready in case Timmons showed up. Some kid got into this, I was just putting it back for you . . .

Magazines, heaps of them, books of photographs—man, *what* photographs! A Calendar for Lovers, rolled up and when unrolled half the size of the front door.

Joe's sister Annie walked by the house on the way to her girl friend's and saw the two boys, seated in the Timmonses' deck chairs, nudging and laughing dirty-joke snorts in their noses.

She joined them, seized a magazine, *Love Lore*, from the box, said, "Honest to God, you ought to be ashamed of yourselves," and started avidly turning the pages.

Mrs. Leary, the head of the Golden Valley Tenants' Association, militant Roman Catholic, mother of four, and self-appointed arbiter of Valley morals and behavior in general, stopped at the foot of the walk on her way to a yard sale on Sunrise Lane.

Later, she said to her husband, "I smelled something wrong, I *smelled* it. Those louts making free of Mr. Timmons' porch, and that trashy girl, you know what a bad influence she is on our Sally . . ."

The look of guilt she got back from the three was all she needed.

"You may be minors," she said, "but trespassing is trespassing." She went quickly up the walk. The first thing her eye fell on was the January picture of A Calendar for Lovers, lying on the all-weather rug, beside Rod Nevins' chair.

To her husband, "I came over faint. The *filth!* Of course I had to look away, but there was a great boxful of it besides what they had in their hands, reading . . ."

The boys, scarlet, shuffled to their feet. Annie with female self-preservation melted around the side of the house.

"A man delivered this and gave me a dollar to watch the stuff," Rod said defiantly. "The box was half open. Told me to watch it till Mr. Timmons came home. So we're, like, watching it." He gave a caw of laughter that didn't come off. "I mean, with little kids and all, this stuff laying around . . ."

"Put everything back in, immediately. Tie up that box, immediately." She saw the address on the flap, Mr. Lester H. Timmons, 2 Rose Road, Golden Valley. Poor Lara, *poor* Lara, and there hadn't been so much as a whisper . . . who would have dreamed that . . . ? And God knows what else, hidden inside the house.

She shooed the cowed boys off. "I'll be watching this porch from my window." She changed her mind about the yard sale, went back to her house, and telephoned around to arrange a small meeting that night of what she thought of as the hard core of the Tenants' Association.

Following his usual practice, Timmons parked his car in a metered slot near the boardwalk and set a fast pace up to the amusement end, ferris wheel, merry-go-round, souvenir shops, popcorn stands, bars. Even now, at ten in the morning, it was crowded and headachingly noisy. Leaning over the rails, studying girls prone on the sand, was a group of dangerous-looking boys in motorcycle helmets and leather jackets with nail-head swastikas embroidered on their backs. Their filthy blue jeans were to Timmons' eye indecently cut.

One of the boys caught his disapproving gaze and burst into a high giggle as he elbowed another boy's side. "Look at Mr. Prim. What don't you like about us, Mr. Prim?"

Timmons turned hastily away, sensing that to insult him, maybe hurt him a little, would be considered fun on this sunny morning. Not allowing himself to glance over his shoulder, look back, he walked rapidly in the opposite direction. His goal was the green pavilion in the far distance. Reach it, turn again, and when he got back to his car he would at least have done a smart mile and a half.

The boardwalk population thinned out as he neared the green pavilion. Two young mothers with two children in strollers. A small boy who might or might not be lost, but the beach police were efficient. So efficient that they were now probably converging on the Nazi-emblemed boys, watching and waiting. Violence often flared, at that now far end of the boardwalk.

He was inhaling an extra-deep lungful of salty air and was enjoying the crisp dry heat striking through his cotton and polyester suit when it happened. A shove from behind into the narrow space between two angle-parked cars, an almost simultaneous crashing feeling in his head, no pain yet, the burn of hot metal against his temple as he fell, and then for a while nothing at all.

It could have been one minute or twenty. He never, later, knew. He opened dazed eyes in darkness—he was halfway under something, oh yes, a car—to hear a woman's voice crying, "Help, *police!*" He was for the moment totally unable to move. A man's voice said, "God, at this hour of the day. Drunk . . . can't you smell it?"

Smell it . . . waves of whiskey fumes floated almost visibly about Timmons' head. A dream, a bad one, but he was waking from it and any time now everything would be all right.

He hit his head on some protrusion underneath the car and fell back on his face again. The pain would stop, too, when the dream ended.

Someone was pulling at his legs. A hard strong tug. He was turned over and hauled to his feet. The blaze of the sun hit him like a fist and his stomach turned over and swaying, he vomited.

"No, no, Carrie, hurry on by, the poor man is sick . . ." A woman with a staring child, her voice echoing from far out beyond the sea, but she was only four feet away from him.

The young policeman who had picked him up asked wearily, "Okay, mister. Name? Address? If you're at it this early in the day we might want to know what you'd get up to later. Better lean against that car before you fall down again. I suppose the heat got you? Or something?"

Timmons rummaged for his handkerchief and mopped his jacket front. His suit seemed to be wet, down the trouser legs. He hadn't—? But one sleeve was wet too.

Obediently supplying his name and address, he added, "Someone hit me from behind," not yet awake and aware enough to put any indignation into his voice. "Shoved me between these two cars and hit me and poured this . . . whatever it is . . . I don't know, maybe one of those boys with the swastikas . . ."

"Wallet missing? Or keys?"

Timmons patted himself. "No."

"I was on my way to that rotten crew when I got sidetracked here," the policeman said, his statement punctuated by a faraway scream and a summoning, piercing police whistle. Hurriedly, he said, "You can report in to the station if you really think someone hit you."

With visions of an item in the local press, and perhaps incarceration in a cell to sober up, Timmons said, "No, no—this kind of thing happens, doesn't it?" still not able to speak clearly.

The young man, not unkind, said, "Look, get yourself a couple cups of coffee, sober up. You planning to drive home in the near future?"

Timmons just barely managed craftiness. "Spending all day

here. With a friend, over there . . ." He nodded toward a row of bald little beach cottages baking in the sun, treeless, grassless, bushless.

"Okay. Can you walk all right now? Good. Got to run," and run he did, up the boardwalk, to the sound of more police whistles.

The sun-steeped metal of the long row of cars was both helpful and painful as he guided himself back to his own car. Got to get out of here, the trouble might soon be over at the other end, the policeman might come back . . .

He allowed himself five minutes of slow deep breathing, sitting behind the wheel. The driving mirror amazed him. No blood, even though his head felt so terrible. The air about him steamed with whiskey.

Take it easy, go slowly, never mind the infuriated horns behind you. Sunlight striking windshields and grilles of cars coming in the opposite direction threatened to blind him, and he had forgotten his dark glasses. Concentrate, hang onto the wheel, take it easy, never mind the . . .

His legs were shaky under him when he put the car into the garage and very slowly got himself out of it. From his Bermuda Porch came a firm command. "Lester! Lester Timmons!"

Timmons had to reach for one of the porch pillars to stay upright. "Yes, Mrs. Leary?"

He didn't think he had ever seen anyone recoil, but that was what Mrs. Leary did. She sniffed, a sniff that could be both seen and heard. "I've been watching this house and this box from my window, waiting for you to show up."

"Why were you watching the box?" Timmons asked, blinking.

"Those books, that filth, half the neighborhood youngsters wallowing in it . . ."

"*What* books?" He swayed a little and tightened his grip on the pillar.

"For the sake of your poor wife, get inside your house, immediately. Some of us are going to want to talk to you when you're in any condition to listen."

Timmons, bewildered by her rage and disgust—she had seemed until this strange morning a nice enough woman—got out his key and fumbled with the lock, then managed it. When he opened the door she bent and shoved the box in after him.

Timmons didn't even bother then to look in the box. He helped himself up his stairway holding onto the (according to the Golden Valley brochure) Spanish Renaissance Wrought Iron Balustrade. He undressed—the suit was washable, he'd throw it into the machine later—took two aspirins and fell onto his bed, and in a minute or two felt himself sinking into sweet blackness.

Lara's call woke him at three. At his sleep-blurred hello her voice sharpened with suspicion. "Were you asleep? You never nap Saturdays." It was she who napped, while he washed the car, Saturday afternoons.

He decided not to tell her right away about the morning, about any of it. Time enough to go into it, when she got home. He couldn't face up to it now and anyway it sounded unreal, crazy, even to him. He said he was just tired.

"Well, Mother's hip is bad and I thought I'd stay on until Tuesday." She intended a surprise return on Monday to see what, if anything, he was up to in her absence. With his new hair dye, and his look of importance, and standing up straighter, and treating himself to a drink not just once in a while but every evening lately . . . as though he was celebrating something.

He showered away the stench of whiskey, put his suit in the washer, and made himself examine the contents of the box in the hall. No identification on the box, no sender, no store name. The few books and magazines he forced himself to glance at weren't new.

What in God's name was it all about?

THIRTEEN

The telex from Switzerland on Friday was nothing to cause any particular concern. Information was wanted on L. H. Timmons.

Security, to which this request was directed, had duplicates of the cards on file with Personnel. Timmons' card noted his rises in salary over his employment span of twenty-five years. Under remarks: Hard worker. Excellent attendance record. Pulls his weight. Slow to attempt innovative approaches to problems. Shows little excitement in the face of challenge. Satisfactory.

But, the message on Monday morning at 10:27:

"From Central Security, Bela Court, Geneva, to McCall, Security, confidential. Two agents Voss and Hoffer arrive Weds for what you will desc as routine security check. Extend fullest coop. You will be briefed on their arrival."

McCall, formerly of the New York police department, had taken early retirement for the much more lucrative and far less dangerous job with Bela. A tub of butter and a bed of roses was the way he saw it. The telex disturbed the peace of his morning and made him a little nervous. He had been gambling heavily and was in pretty deep; suppose Security checked Security? They might not approve of the people he had to turn to for money. ". . . what you will describe as a routine check." . . . So it wasn't routine.

Worry shared is worry halved, his mother used to say. He handed the telex to Wade, his assistant. "What the hell do you make of this?"

Janie Daley had just come into the little outer office where employees whom McCall and Wade had reason to talk to were allowed to cool their heels. Her visit was social: the exchange of good mornings with handsome Wade.

"Well, there was that thing on Friday, wanting Timmons' record," Wade said. "I took care of it."

The door to the inner office was a foot or so open. Janie stood still and held her breath, listening.

"Who again is Timmons?"

From his computer memory, Wade produced, "Merchandising, Promotion, etcet. We talked to him some time last month, the day after that girl's office was torn up. He'd come back up the night before for his rubbers. But nothing much to go on, said he'd been in the men's room a while. He's always been a good little boy according to Personnel."

The culprit had never been discovered. The matter had been quietly shelved.

Still nervous, McCall said, "You can't tell me they'd send two men all the way from Switzerland to look into some spilled ink and a few overturned filing cabinets. We didn't even report it to them. Doesn't look good when it's left open-ended."

"Maybe somebody else did. And remember there was that nut in Brazil who set the fire." Wade's own conscience was clear and he looked forward to some excitement in this Jersey backwater. International matters, maybe.

Janie moved silently out into the corridor and then began to walk very rapidly down it. One in the eye for Veronica Kovach, who always thought she was the first to hear what was going on.

The word crept through various Bela buildings like a tremor. "I heard . . ." ". . . But don't say you heard it from *me* . . ." "Yes, Wednesday . . ."

Veronica put down her phone and swiveled around in her chair. Her hard-boiled egg and her apple were temporarily forgotten. Wide-eyed, she said, "My God, Les, you did it!"

"Did what–?"

"They're coming, detectives, police, whatever they are, all the way from Switzerland."

Timmons was planning to answer in a cool way, "Well, naturally," but found he had no breath at all. He sat in a daze of bliss and astonishment, staring ahead of him, seeing nothing, in the lunchtime-emptied pool. His phone rang.

A secretarial voice–he lost the name–said, "Mr. Timmons, we'd just love it if Mrs. Timmons would like to sit in at a meeting tonight of the new Bela Big Sisters? Wives of employees are more than welcome. I tried to get her at your home number, but maybe she's out shopping–"

Dreamily, Timmons said, "She's away from home, sorry, won't be back until tomorrow, but thank you anyway, perhaps the next meeting . . ."

Charlie Corleone called Ralph Horner at two. "You heard? The little bastard's gone and done it. Whaddya say we turn on Operation Cheryl today? This afternoon. No harm trying."

Horner had indeed heard, and ten seconds later had kicked his wastebasket hard and high; it just missed Joe Beadon's shoulder. "I'll call her," he said, and one hand clutched the other in gleeful fashion before he began dialing.

Cheryl was nineteen. Right now her last name was Lavallette. She found it convenient to give herself new first and surnames from time to time. She was tall and thin but generously breasted. Her hair was worn in a pinkish-yellow afro, usually showing dark at the roots. Her skin was an odd greenish-beige but she wore a great deal of translucent makeup; still, the color showed on the parts of her that were bare.

The long-dead mini was alive and well among those following Cheryl's calling. This afternoon, she wore a fitted silver-pink satin dress that brushed the tops of her thighs and, hot as it was, silver foil-finished plastic boots that came up over her knees.

Her obliging male friend from the boardwalk dropped her in front of Timmons' house and said, "Yell if they start throwing stones at you. I'll only be a couple blocks away," and drove off.

Those two nice men who were going to give her fifty dollars for this had rehearsed her carefully. She strolled up the cement walk, busily chewing gum. She turned and settled herself in one of the deck chairs, lazily locked her hands behind her afro, and stretched her long silver boots in front of her. Every so often, she would lean forward and gaze intently to her left and right. Expectantly. Waiting. Yawning, settling back again.

Cars going by slowed to study her. She was unmistakable; she out-whored the more flamboyant of the Golden Valley girls by a mile.

A man emerged from the next house, on the left, and ambled over to a flower border where he squatted down and started to pull little weeds among the zinnias and marigolds. Cheryl wandered to the low fence dividing the two properties.

"Hey," she said. The man, who hadn't until now observed her, looked up and almost fell over backward; his arm shot behind him to support him. From this awkward position he gaped up at Cheryl.

"Hey, do you know when Timmsy is expected home? Mr. Timmons, I mean. I usually see him at my place, but he wanted me here today—wants to show me his shell collection." And she winked one large dark eye at the Timmonses' neighbor, Mr. Parker.

He was so alarmed and startled—any moment now, his wife might look out of the window and see him talking to this . . . this—that he struggled to his feet and headed rapidly for his front door, turning once to look over his shoulder as though fearful of pursuit.

Inside the house, he said to his wife, "Quick, the window—look what Les's got on his front porch."

Mrs. Parker obeyed and stared eagerly as the sprawled

pink-and-silver girl languidly inserted a cigarette into a long holder and lit it. There were butts on the flagstones all around her chair.

"I'll go borrow a cup of rice from Madge," she said. Madge Hingham lived in the house on the other side of Number 2.

At the foot of the walk, Mrs. Parker stopped and called, "Were you waiting for someone? I'm sure you've got the wrong—"

"No, I haven't got the wrong anything," Cheryl said. "I'm waiting for Timmsy. Mr. Timmons." There was a silver chain around her neck that dangled into the plunging collar of her dress. She reached under the collar, between her breasts—no bra, of course, the appalled Mrs. Parker noted—and hauled out a round silver watch and studied it. "No later than five-fifteen, he said, and it's five-twenty now."

"*Mr.* Timmons never comes home until five-thirty at the earliest," Mrs. Parker informed her, not moving from the sidewalk a step nearer to this frightful girl. Even from here she could smell the heavy perfume, seeming to come at her in waves.

"Oh well, he gets excited, you know how it is. Maybe he got his times mixed up . . ."

Outraged, Mrs. Parker went on to Number Three and had to wait a little before the doorbell was answered because, as she found out right away, Madge Hingham could hardly pry herself away from the window. They both stood, watching.

At 5:25, the girl rose and gave a haughty, impatient toss of her head. She reached into her silver handbag, took out a piece of paper, held it against the door, wrote something on it, and fastened it to the door with a piece of plastic tape. Then, hips in professional action, satin swinging, she went down the walk, raised a signaling arm, and was a minute later picked up by a car, not Timmons', an anonymous old gray car.

Timmons arrived home at 5:55. As usual, he put his car in the garage and went through into the kitchen, thereby missing the note on his front door.

Along with moral indignation, various bigotries were aired over Golden Valley dinner tables.

"She looked like a spick to me," said Mr. Parker. "Besides the other thing, I mean."

Spooning canned beef gravy over the mashed potatoes, Madge Hingham said to her husband, ". . . a ton of make-up on her face but the arms, and those great naked . . . upper legs . . . a mulatto, or rather a black I suppose you'd say . . ."

Mrs. Cantor, whose car going by was one of those that had slowed, whispered to Mr. Cantor, "I'll tell you more about it later, here comes Buddy now. But anyway, Italian, maybe, you get that swarthy color sometimes with Italians . . . or Greeks . . ." "You wouldn't know a hooker if you fell over one," laughed Mr. Cantor. "Oh yes I would, she might as well have had a For Rent sign on her . . . ssshh. Hurry up, sit down, Buddy, your soup's getting cold."

Mrs. Leary was informed of the visitor by no less than four people. "Well, after those books, that *filth* . . . but Lester Timmons, Lester *Timmons*. Although you do hear that sometimes it's the ones that look the properest and the quietest are up to the most terrible things. I'm sure I don't know who's going to get up the courage to tell Lara. I suppose it will end up being me."

What made Timmons late getting home was a stopover at Oliver's on the way. At least, he hoped Oliver would be there; he had had a morning meeting in New York.

Without Oliver's near presence in the office, this afternoon, he had felt a little like a boat adrift, lacking an anchor. He had never remembered the pool so silent. People working, or looking as though they were working, not talking very much and when they did their voices were low. Hardly anyone spoke to him; of course, they'd all know it by now. He tried hard to hang onto his feeling of heady triumph.

During the afternoon coffee break, Joe Beadon stopped at his desk and said, "Well, all ready, Les? Will in order? Affairs all tidied up?" with a sour grin.

"Don't be ridiculous," Timmons said, flushing.

"It's sure been nice knowing you. I want you to know you'll be missed," Beadon said. "Can I buy you a last cup of coffee?"

To get away from him, Timmons went over to the water cooler, and on the way realized that his throat was quite dry.

Mabel Kovarski was standing beside the water cooler. She watched him as he filled a little white cup. Her narrowed golden gaze reminded him of that long, long look across the pool when the guards had been questioning him about Marie Eggena's office.

Very slowly, she said, "And have you put your own self on your list, Les? Somebody said, I forget who, that for a while they thought you messed up Eggena's office, when you came back up here for your rubbers. And they haven't found out yet who did it. Yes, I think you belong on the list."

Taken off guard, Timmons said, "But, *Mabel*–" and then felt his heart give a curious thump as the dark golden eyes widened and widened, and held his own so that he felt totally unable to look away from them. There was some kind of movement, thinning, of her nostrils, a white pinching. She lifted her shoulders in a long sigh and very quietly and without another word turned away from him and went back to her desk.

Yes, catch Oliver up on things, and tell him about the inexplicable madnesses on Saturday.

Driving in behind the house, he saw a leggy attractive young woman in shorts and a yellow shirt reading under a tree. She got up and came over to the car. "Yes?"

"I'm Lester Timmons. I wondered if Oliver was home yet–I'd like to see him."

He was aware of a fascinated interest in the long merry blue eyes. "No, he's not back, but might be any minute, would you like to wait?" And then, and he felt a further quickening of interest, "Perhaps you'll join me in a drink while you wait? I'm just about to have one. In a way we know each other, Oliver talks, naturally, about the . . . people he knows at Bela."

She wasn't by any means Oliver, but her friendliness and ease, and her having nothing at all to do with Bela, in a way comforted him.

"If it's not an imposition . . . ?" He was still obscurely shaken.

"Can I buy you a last cup of coffee?" And Mabel's eyes timelessly going wider. It took him a little while to figure out why she had asked him if he'd put himself on the list, but with another heart thump it hit him: to find out if he had seen her that night. And, before taking time to think, he had as much as told her: yes, he had.

"Follow me," Lou said, after having introduced herself. "It's cooler inside." Timmons had forgotten about winter porches, where clothes could be dried in cold weather, and wood stored. He waited as she tried the knob, made a small impatient sound—"Lock's snicked itself"—and reached to tip up an empty clay flowerpot on a broad white catchall table and got a key out from under it. She was right, it was cooler inside. A breeze lifted the white curtains at one of the kitchen windows.

"Yes, whiskey, thanks, or anything you have, anything at all." To make conversation, he added, "I thought Oliver said you worked in New York?"

After her perhaps three seconds in Oliver's arms yesterday, Lou had decided immediately to take her vacation from here on in in long weekends. Yes, entirely sensible, and think of the money to be saved by not going to London in October.

Besides, her apartment was being painted, today and tomorrow, and it suddenly occurred to her that she couldn't face *that* mess. By telephone this morning she had offered her cleaning woman an enormous bribe to come in after the disaster and see that everything was in perfect order before she returned.

She explained the stretched weekend, and the painting, to Timmons as he sipped his drink and looked around her room, and felt himself in another world that held gaiety and a warming charm.

"It's nice here," he said shyly, surprising himself. "I wish—"

Just in time he caught himself. Not that in any case he would have finished the vague, longing uprush, would he? I wish I were Oliver and that someone like you was my wife and I lived in this house. I'm sure I'd be another kind of man entirely.

Not Lester Timmons.

Seeing his sudden color, Lou broke a silence of several minutes. She asked him casually if there was anything interesting going on at Bela. He said no, August was usually a slack month there, and then looked to her as though he wanted to tell her something, and wasn't able to.

He stretched his drink and his visit to twenty minutes. He was aware that she was listening too, waiting too, for Oliver. "Well, I won't put you out any longer . . . you've been most kind . . ."

Getting up, he turned in the wrong direction and found himself facing what must be a cellar door, in the little hall outside the room. Why, Timmons thought distractedly, do I always go the wrong way out of any room?

"No, this way . . ." and she made pleasant nice-to-meet-you noises.

In the doorway to the back yard, he turned. "If you by any chance happen to see Oliver"—delicately, mustn't imply things, intimacy, an unattached man and this taking kind of girl, just the two of them in the house—"will you tell him it's happened, and that they're coming? He'll know what I mean." He paused, and said again, "Tell him they're coming."

FOURTEEN

They're coming, Timmons said to himself as he toasted white bread and spread it with sardines in tomato sauce. Too hot to eat a large meal, but Sunday afternoon he had bought cantaloupes and peaches. He halved a cantaloupe and scooped the seeds into the garbage can with its neat plastic bag lining. Lara, tomorrow, would have no grounds for scolding about his housekeeping; the kitchen was clean and after his shopping he had done the floor with the sponge mop.

They're coming.

He had seen in a last year's issue of *Fortune* magazine photographs of exteriors and interiors at Bela Court. Teak walls, impossibly tall gilded doorways, tapestries, Persian rugs, the visible ordered hush of money and power. He heard, mentally, whispers exchanged in the doorways. That American, that Timmons—*mon Dieu*, what a man! What an eye! What a nose! Perhaps a good thing that *we* don't have a Timmons here . . . Admiring, complimenting laughter.

After his dinner, he made himself a drink with a double jigger of Four Roses and took it into the living room. He didn't want to watch television. He wanted to watch himself, already a man of legend at Bela Court. He had never been to Switzerland, or anywhere abroad. He and Lara had had three moderately long-distance trips: Yosemite National Park, Miami out of season one year, insufferably hot, and Montreal for Expo '67.

What would they do, when they found out it was all true? Promote him, surely. What job would he like, when they asked him? Personnel head? Office manager? Surely something bigger and better than those two. A new post, perhaps a new title, head of Liaison. Our man at Bela. Divide your time, Mr. Timmons, between the New Jersey and Texas offices, and of course we'll want you to allow a few months for Brazil and Brussels and Berlin and Florence. You'll be far above Security status, reporting only to Bela Court. On the surface, you're a very special branch of Public Relations, that will be your cover.

How ridiculous, now, those afternoon slivers of fear. There was no point in doing anything to *him* now that the information was in their hands. All they had to do now was dig on their own to substantiate his—complaints was the wrong word—succinct little dossiers.

Except . . . there were a few things to which he had been the only witness. Mabel Kovarski's destructive passion, for one.

He found his glass empty well before it should be, and went to get another drink. Surely a night for celebration, and today there had been nobody to celebrate with. Even Veronica, after lunch, had turned odd, cool. She had spent her afternoon far away from his desk, helping the new girl flounder through her first booklet, on HairBreeze, The Lotion that Lifts Your Hair Like Flying Silk on the Summer Wind.

Liaison Head . . . I'll want reservations, Miss Somebody, get me on a plane for Rio early tomorrow, first class . . . the Hilton will do nicely, and I'll need a suite as there are various people I must interview in privacy . . .

The Hilton turned into a big bare room full of shouting accusing voices. Joe Beadon handed him a cup of coffee and said, "Here, drink this, it won't hurt you but it's your last cup of coffee, it's been nice knowing you . . ."

Timmons jerked awake. How long had he been asleep? Not long, it was close to ten, and he had a reassuring half drink left. Well, excitement is tiring. Breathing the heady air on top of the world is tiring. Walking a tightrope is tiring—but how had that image come into his head?

There was a light knock at the door. He applied his eye to

the peeker without success; the Tenants' Association had decreed that porch lights be turned off at 9:30 to conserve energy. The bold new Liaison Head opened the door a few inches.

Kalish gave it a gentle authoritative push inward and walked into the hall, closing the door behind him.

"Happened to be in the neighborhood and thought I'd drop by," he explained, going into the living room after thriftily switching off the hall light. He stood in the center of the room, looking around, at Lara's cretonnes and bronze wall plaques of birds, her rose-patterned beige rug and her cactus collection.

"Trim little place you have here. Cheery." The off-duty Kalish was casually dressed in a black turtleneck jersey and slender black pants. He took off his dark glasses and placed them on the coffee table and in doing so spotted Timmons' drink.

Entirely bewildered for the moment with this visit, and this unlikely visitor, Timmons' first thought was, That will go onto my record card: Timmons is given to drinking alone.

"Care for a drop?" Hating the eagerness in his voice, low man to higher-up.

Kalish, with an air of absentmindness, began drawing the cretonne curtains on their traverse rods.

"Wouldn't do for anyone to spot us, in conference, you might call it," he said over a broad shoulder. In this black outfit, Timmons thought, he looks bigger, taller than he does at the office.

In conference. Potent words. Kalish coming to confer with him. Thinking his audience with Lester Timmons so important, so secret, that he was taking no chance with possibly prying eyes.

"Now I'll join you in a drink." Not thankfully accepting hospitality, but conveying a favor. He looked at his watch. "We haven't a great deal of time."

"We?" Oh yes, he and his fellow conferee.

He followed Timmons into the kitchen and drew the curtains there while Timmons poured a too-hefty drink for him, not wanting to be thought stingy.

As they left the kitchen, Kalish considerately snapped off the overhead light.

Lara had had every intention of arriving home, unannounced, around eight o'clock, but Frank Rainer festively changed her plans. He called her at her mother's in the early afternoon and said he was in Goodwood, and would be there just for this one night, and could he see her.

Lara said hungrily, "I don't know . . . I'd planned to be home sometime after dinner . . ."

"You *will* be home sometime after dinner, our dinner and then a little loving get-together here in the motel." They discussed the bus schedule. He would pick her up at Lakewood and drop her off near home later.

After her third manhattan, she confided, "This sounds funny, coming from me, but I was kind of sneaking home a day early to see if he's up to anything. I swear I think he's begun playing around . . ."

"Well, tit for tat, if you know what I mean," Frank leered happily, "but he doesn't look to me like the great lover. Speaking of that, hurry up and finish your steak. I'll get you there at ten or so and you might even catch them in the act."

Kalish sat, lightly poised, on the end of the sofa. As he lit a cigarette, Timmons noticed that he had round Band-Aids on the balls of his thumb and forefinger.

"Cut yourself or something?" he asked politely.

"A matchbook went off in my hand, minor casualties," Kalish said. "By the way, d'you have a cocktail napkin or something? I don't want to leave rings on your table."

"Oh, sorry, living a bachelor life you forget the—" Timmons went into the kitchen. Better not turn on the overhead light, fluorescents swallowed a great gulp of energy when switched on. Kalish might think him careless, extravagant. In the dim light from the living room, he found a paper napkin with "Cheers!" scrawled all over it.

"Thanks." Kalish neatly folded the napkin about his glass and took a leisurely sip. Timmons waited patiently for the conference to begin. His eyes followed Kalish's gaze, to the doorknob with his suit jacket and tie hung over it, a liberty Lara would never have allowed.

His head felt funny. The unaccustomed amount to drink, perhaps, the immensity of his achievement. He had the strangest feeling that Kalish was in some secret way enjoying himself.

"Hot night," he said apologetically, waving at the tie and jacket. "I don't like to turn up the air conditioning too high, the electric bills are—"

"*Sssshh!*" Kalish hissed suddenly. "Did I hear someone? Better not take any chances."

He got up and went swiftly round the room, switching off lamps.

Fear, which might have been there, way down underneath, all the time, caught Timmons in a wave, at first cold and then sweating hot.

He didn't want to be alone in the deep, unrelieved dark with Ronald Kalish.

"It's okay, I think," Kalish murmured after what might have been a minute or two but seemed much longer. "Where's your bathroom, by the way? Upstairs? Mind if I borrow it? Just for safety leave the lights off until I come back down."

Safety from *what?* Did Kalish suspect someone might be following him, to see if he made contact with the suddenly all-important Lester Timmons?

His having to attend to a normal human function took away a little of the gathering fear. But Timmons defiantly turned on the light at his end of the sofa and gulped so desperately at his half drink that he choked and began coughing.

Kalish ran down the stairs and switched off the lamp again. "I think I saw someone leaning against a lamppost a good way down the block. Might have been Ralph Horner. Crazy bastard might be planning to set your house on fire after the neighbors go to bed, you know his temper—"

A sense of swift motion in the dark, the breeze of it hitting Timmons' hot wet face. A hand on one shoulder, and then something around his neck—

He tried to get up. The hand was over his mouth now, clampingly cruel, and in his struggling he was flung face-down on the sofa and the hand was removed and the pressure on his neck was agonizingly increased.

Dim against dark, Lara saw the note on the door and pulled it off and put it in her pocket. Funny, the lights out but the car in the garage. He didn't usually go to bed this early. Unless right this moment, right in her house, he had the nerve to be—

A strong reek of perfume rising from the deck chair assailed her nose.

Her key turned silently in the lock, which Timmons kept well oiled. She tiptoed into the hall and in the darkness nearby heard a kind of grunting and thrashing and gasping.

Her own fresh guilt, and the weeks of wondering about her rejuvenated husband, had preconditioned her and dictated her swift enraged reaction.

On *her* sofa, in *her* living room—

From the doorway, she cried imperiously, *"Lester Timmons!"*

The thrashing and grunting assumed a lowered weight and volume, and then she simultanously apprehended an inhuman sawing half-sobbing sound and felt something coming at her.

She was savagely struck in the face by a fist and the blow flung her backward. Her head hit the edge of the bottom step of the stairway, and she thought she heard herself screaming, but then the pouring noise in her throat was no longer audible to her.

Just before her blackout, she thought there was in this pain-thudding nowhere the sound of the back door, closing.

When she came to, she returned to her screaming, slowly at first, and then in hysteria, wondering if her neck was broken, if she had concussion, if she was maybe dying here in the hall. The darkness—

She reached back a hand to her head and felt it wet. Panic forced her to try to get up out of the blood, the horror. Her hand found the wrought iron banister post and she hauled herself to her feet.

An undersized blackamoor on the post held a globe with a dim bulb in it. Almost falling against the near wall, she found the switch and saw when the light came on scarlet smears around the switch panel, all over her nice clean beige-painted wall.

"Lara . . . ?" A quack, or a croak, from the living room.

She fell on her hands and knees in the doorway, only half seeing the prone body on the sofa trying to lift its head.

"She almost killed me, she may have killed me, I may be bleeding to death," Lara shouted, and started screaming again.

FIFTEEN

As Parker was to tell it later, and widely:

"Well. You never saw such a sight. She was all bleeding, and she had his suit jacket over her head with the sleeves tied under her chin, trying to stop the blood I suppose, or sop it up —and he was on the couch with his head hanging almost between his knees, and there was an empty glass beside him, and when I got close I smelled the booze—"

The screaming had brought Parker and his wife to the Timmonses' door. Parker put his finger on the bell and kept it there.

As though there was no ringing all through the house, no one there but himself, Timmons mumbled into the hands locked over his face, "He, he . . ."

"*He?*" You mean, *she* . . . *!*"

He became aware of someone in the slipper chair, facing him. Yes, Lara, but what was that over and around her head? The light from the hall showed him a nightmare face with blood on its cheek.

"Somebody should answer the door."

A thin voice, maybe his own, maybe hers.

Parker, stating the opinion which became that of Golden Valley: "She managed to get to the door and let us in. We figured she wouldn't have, except she needed a doctor and he was in no shape to help her. That tart . . . Timmsy, she called him . . . Lara must have found them and *she* ran off and they had a fight and Timmons beat her up. He kept muttering some craziness about someone trying to kill *him*, to cover up I guess . . ."

"Call Ben," he said to his stunned wife, and she went to the telephone and dialed Dr. Benjamin Mossman, their son-in-law, who lived six blocks away on Peony Lane. And then, her other answer to any emergency, "Perhaps I should go and make some coffee . . ."

Timmons' strange naked face, from which he had now removed his hands, frightened her.

From his far plateau, he said, "I have been nearly murdered." He sounded as though he didn't quite believe, yet, that he was alive. "With my own tie, off the doorknob—here it is." He held up the dark green tie. "Around my throat, choking me to death."

"D'you suppose it was that girl?" Mrs. Parker asked of the air. "Robbery, maybe—have you checked your wallet?"

"What girl?" Lara asked blurrily, from her chair.

"A girl in pink satin and silver boots, waiting outside your door for him, although I don't know that I ought to . . . you've already had a shock . . ."

"She called him Timmsy," Parker said. "I think we could all use some coffee, Mother." But Mrs. Parker, listening, found herself unable to move.

"Just before he did it he went upstairs, he wanted the bathroom, but now I remember there wasn't any sound of the toilet flushing. I think he might have wanted to see if there was a hook on the back of the door. I think he might have been going to hang me on the hook in my own bathroom." Timmons touched his neck tenderly as if to make sure it was still there, still working. "There *is* a hook, a good strong one, I put it on myself, it didn't come with the house . . .

"Or," Timmons said to his knees, "if it wasn't high enough—I've never tried hanging myself on it, I wouldn't know—he could drive me off in my own car, nobody'd see him with the body, going through the kitchen, and then dump me somewhere . . ."

The doorbell rang and Parker admitted Dr. Mossman.

"Family matter," he said. "Mrs. Timmons has been struck on the head, you can see she's—"

"I think somebody ought to call the police, people can't murder people in their own houses," Timmons said patiently.

Back turned to him, Parker showed the doctor a glass-draining gesture in explanation.

"If you'll get off the sofa," Mossman said briskly. "I'll want it for the patient."

But Timmons couldn't get up and when Parker went to enforce the order and lifted him the other man's legs sagged and he fell to his knees.

Paying no attention to him, Mossman helped Lara to the sofa, removed her large impromptu bandage, and examined the wound at the back of her head. She was moaning, partly with pain, partly with drenching shame. All these people, seeing and hearing . . .

The disgrace of it. Waiting for him, in silver boots. The perfume, out there on the porch. Timmsy.

"Nothing to cry about, Mrs. Timmons," Mossman said. "I think it's all right, but I'll want an X ray and then you'll need a few stitches. Call an ambulance, Dad, Walker Memorial, and tell them I'll want a bed for her overnight."

Couldn't leave her here with this collapsed mumbling man down on his hands and knees. Family matter . . . and she pretty helpless what with the loss of blood and the shock of the attack.

"Get up, Les, do," implored Mrs. Parker. "It doesn't look—"

Timmons addressed himself to a large cabbage rose in the carpet, a foot below his dangling head.

Continuing the explanation which in this new, mad world, nobody would pay any attention to, nobody seemed to believe —*why?*—he said, "She must have sneaked home a day early thinking she'd catch me out in something. I don't know what. She saved my life."

The telephone rang and Lara said, hopelessly but pleadingly, while her head was being bandaged, "Please don't let anyone—please don't tell anyone, *please*—"

Madge Hingham shrilled to Parker, "I thought I heard

screams, or was it the TV? And then when the doctor's car stopped outside . . ."

"I can't talk now, but everything's under control," Parker said, with Lara's dark eyes boring holes in him.

Time passed while they waited for the ambulance. Mrs. Parker made the coffee and served it. Parker had gotten Timmons up off the floor, and onto the slipper chair. He looked green and ill and was silent, as though his assaulted throat was incapable of producing any more sounds.

Particularly when nobody, nobody at all, would listen.

Even though he'd been nearly murdered.

The ambulance made its approach known. Lara fumbled in her pocket, got out the note she had pulled off the door in some distant half remembered time and unthinkingly read it aloud. "See you a little later, lover, yours, Cheryl."

"Now we're feeling better and able to walk, aren't we," Mossman said cheerily, helping her to her feet. "Off we go to the hospital."

Lara refastened her eyes on Parker. "Don't you let him call the police. God, maybe she did try to strangle him for his money . . . it's bad enough *you* knowing, but if it got into the papers or anything . . . I swear I'd kill myself."

The door closed behind them. Mrs. Parker collected coffee cups and looked with horrified distaste at Timmons, who hadn't touched his cup. To her husband, she said, "Well, getting on for bedtime."

Timmons roused himself. "You're not going to leave me alone, are you?"

"Alone? Well, as you heard, Lara's going to have a night in the hospital. She'll be fine tomorrow, probably, a few stitches and then . . ."

"But he may come back and try to kill me all over again."

Parker's safeguarding mind totally rejected the idea of a murderer loose in nice quiet Golden Valley. "Well, see you're locked up nice and tight," he said soothingly. He felt that he had had enough and more than enough of the Timmonses' problems. He wanted his hot cocoa and the "Late Show."

The slow tears trickling out of Timmons' eyes and down alongside his nose sent both husband and wife out the front door in a hurry.

"He wasn't just drinking Four Roses, it must have been *Five* Roses," Mrs. Parker said. "Tess Leary swears they're going to vote him right out of here, but poor Lara . . ."

". . . or mental, maybe." Parker shook his head. "Like Uncle Wilfred. Remember? He went off to take his afternoon nap sane and woke up crazy."

In the leaden quiet of aftershock, in steady desperation, Timmons at close to midnight called Oliver.

After three rings, the call was answered.

"Oliver. Pardon the tonsils, I can't speak very well because—"

"So much the better," a tired cool voice informed him.

"I'm alone here, I'm worried. There's been horrible trouble. Somebody hit Lara, and as if that wasn't bad enough, and before that, I mean, they tried to—"

Oliver cut crisply across the fumbling words.

"As of this past weekend, when someone of yours tried to fix *me* one way or another, I'm no longer your trustee, Les. Or confidant. You're strictly on your own."

"But, Oliver—"

A waste of the voice, which was now difficult to produce from a burning throat; the clean buzz of a disconnected line.

The stairs were an obvious impossibility. Timmons forced himself, in slow motion, to check the locks on the doors and the latches on the ground floor windows. Then he made the distance to the sofa, and after a while managed to pull down a kind of mental blind. Too much to be borne, so you didn't bear it; but gave yourself over to the welcome blank death of sleep.

SIXTEEN

Lou, reading in bed, heard Oliver come in and go up his stairs at a little before eleven. She hadn't told him she was going to stay on a few more days because that would be assuming, on his part, a minute-to-minute interest in her comings and goings.

But he couldn't not have noticed her bedroom windows lighted, facing the porch. Strange that the arriving feet of the unaccountably most important person in one's world could go lightly upward, strange that there wasn't even a casual good night called from the porch.

Thumping her pillow furiously, she thought, I'll sell this place, this goddamned Circe place, this rival, this love of his—

Forget it, Lou. To borrow a word from your grandmother, you're daft. But deliver the almost-forgotten message from Timmons, using his own cool good manners to do so.

Oliver had been taken aback at his own rush of surprise and pleasure, warmth, when he had seen the ground-floor lights on at Lou's. It was like having forgotten, leaving your house, you had left your radio on and being startled on re-entering by a burst of festive music.

He looked at his watch in the glow from the near window. She could have fallen asleep with the lights on. He heard again the sweet waking voice floating out to him. "Oliver . . ." and "I was dreaming . . . ." No, not a good idea, not at this hour, not Lou in bed, perhaps tousled with sleeping and looking as she had to Finch delightfully inefficient. After the moment of hesitation, he unlocked his front door.

He was half undressed when Timmons' call came. He had made up his mind Saturday night that he would immediately and firmly extricate himself from Timmons' embroilments, but when he hung up he felt a little guilty. Oh well, somebody had hit his wife, but there was no ensuing announcement of her demise, and presumably the same somebody had tried to do something else, unspecified because he had crisply cut Timmons off. The try couldn't have worked, whatever it was, because Timmons was alive and functioning even if sounding a bit gasping and racked in the voice.

No doubt it would be all over the office in the morning; he'd be favored with the story by Veronica, probably, if Timmons got the message and left him alone.

The telephone rang again as he poured himself a drink. With another curt refusal at the ready, he answered it and heard Lou's not at all sleepy voice.

"Sorry to call you at this unlikely hour, but I have a message for you—"

Before he could stop himself, he said, "*Lou.* When I saw your lights on I thought Santa Claus had come five months early."

There was an odd little pause and then the sigh of an expelled breath. "My apartment's being painted," she explained. "Well, anyway, your Timmons stopped around wanting to see you and left this message which sounds to me a bit apocalyptic. 'It's happened and they're coming, he'll know what I mean.'"

"For God's sake," he burst out angrily, "I don't want you to have anything to do with him."

At first taking this as a directive to stay out of his affairs, she said, "Well, the man drove into the back yard looking for you," leaving out her own ardent curiosity, and the shared drinks to indulge it.

"I'm sorry, Lou, I don't think you understood me . . . he's harmless in himself, but he's a sort of walking Typhoid Mary, and the less you know about him, the less contact you have with him, the better."

"It had," she said slowly, "crossed my mind that his envelopes, his lists, might have had something to do with what happened to you Saturday night . . ."

"You know nothing about any list, and he was and is from now on, a total stranger to you," Oliver said. "Good night, Lou darling."

Timmons' night was not disturbed further except by terrible dreams and sweating awakenings, in one of which he heard himself crying out.

In the morning, his knees wouldn't support him in the shower so he changed the shower to a bath. His neck looked awful, grayed purple and green with stormy patches of red at the front. He was wincingly experimenting with Lara's liquid make-up, a pinky-beige color, when the bedside phone summoned him.

I should stay home, with this neck, he thought on the way to answer it, but I'm afraid to stay home. I want people, a lot of people, around me.

Lara said, "Come and get me, Les, they want my bed. She —didn't come back, did she?"

"Nobody came back." It struck him as almost equally grotesque that Kalish should try to kill him in his own house and that nobody would pay the smallest attention to this appalling truth. "I'll get a cup of coffee and be right over, Lara, and then we've got to talk."

"Your voice sounds horrible . . . well, hurry."

Backing out the short driveway, he saw the wreath on the door and got out of the car and went to examine it. Big, three feet across, white crysanthemums and grape leaves wired into it. A broad white satin ribbon across the center, on which had been lettered boldly, "Lester H. Timmons. Rest in peace."

He snatched it off the door and took it to the car, not looking to the left or right. If anyone asked, he'd say it was a congratulatory gesture to mark the anniversary of his twenty-five years with Bela. That is, unless early pedestrians and sharp-eyed drivers had already read the ribbon.

Rest in peace. Not Kalish, Kalish with his lights-out and commands for silence. Kalish wouldn't be advertising him on his own front door.

I can't cope, I can't think, I can't handle more than one thing at once, Timmons told himself, wanting again to burst into tears. Crossing the bridge over Farms River on the way to the hospital, he stopped the car off the road on the far side, got out, and tossed the wreath into the water. There, it's gone, and don't tell Lara, ever.

"Les?" In the car, she looked over at him. "I must say your neck looks awful, worse than your voice. They gave me a pill last night but I was thinking, doing a lot of thinking. They, the Parkers, kept saying she and you kept saying he. *Promise* me you won't go to the police about it. Jesus, Les, if it all came out—"

Timmons suddenly felt like a man who had waked to a dismal hangover and then getting on his feet began to feel the excitement of the alcohol in his veins again, floating him slightly off the ground.

"Naturally, I won't go to the police if you don't mind being a widow." The wreath, and Lara's head all but split open, and his guest, the great Kalish, the $40,000-a-year Kalish, zeroing on *him*, so frightened of what Lester Timmons could do to him that the only thing to do was kill him. After all the giggles, and the taunts, and, "What number are you up to now, Les?"

They're coming. Save it for their ears? It would make real sense to *them*. And his waiting, holding back—a kind of club poised over Kalish's head.

"Don't talk that way. Widow! But, I mean, the police, it will have to come out about that tramp waiting for you on the porch, while your wife was away . . ."

With a sudden glimmering, Timmons added to himself, Yes, and the pornographic books delivered, and me being thought drunk and disorderly on the boardwalk. Maybe the police wouldn't even take his tale seriously? No witnesses . . .

Offhandedly, he said, "It was Kalish who tried to kill me. I thought some during the night too, and what I had on him was enough to get him fired, I suppose, but then I wondered if there was something bigger and worse he thought they might stumble onto when they were looking into him and his young men . . ."

A memory came back, summoned by his own words. Bert Orrin in New York, a slim elegant boy, one of Kalish's, they said. One morning Bert Orrin hadn't turned up for work and there was a brief flurry of excitement when it was found that he had just plain disappeared. For good, it turned out.

It had occurred to Lara in her hospital bed that if the evening and night were looked into by the police, the question might come up of where she was and what she had been doing from the time she left her mother's to the moment of silently unlocking the door at 2 Rose Lane. She'd heard they always thought of the spouse first.

If they found out—if not only he, but *she* was to be dragged in the mud, smeared with it, for all the world to see—her mind closed against the awfulness.

"Promise me, promise me, Les. If it *was* Kalish, maybe he went black for a moment, or something, maybe he was drunk, maybe he had some kind of nervous fit. Look, if he tries anything, anything at all, like firing you to get you off his back, I'll get Ellen Parker to describe him, like his own photograph, say she'd seen him going out our back door."

Her voice, bargaining, made a conscientious attempt to accept Kalish as his possible attacker. The threat to herself loomed, now, far larger.

Up and fighting again, if feeling slightly out of focus, Timmons said, "Not a bad idea . . . by the way, you'll be packing a bag as soon as you get home." It felt good, giving orders to Lara.

"Why on earth—?"

"To go to your mother's. It's too dangerous for you here. It's my duty to tell you that I did send that list. To Switzerland. And people are coming over to look into things. Because of the list." In an odd way, it now seemed all gloriously worthwhile.

Lara held back the harridan arguments that leaped to her throat.

If he'd agree to shut up, so that the pink-and-silver girl wouldn't be in all the papers, and the police wouldn't be poking around to see what the spouse was up to before she belatedly got home . . . God, they might even gang up on Frank. His car, dropping her, could have been seen in the vicinity. Jealous lover tries to strangle paramour's husband . . .

"Okay. I think you're crazy, but what's done's done." Placatingly, pressing the advantage, "Who knows, you might even get something out of it. A promotion or something."

"I might indeed," said Timmons.

After dropping Lara at the bus station—"Yes, Lara, I'll call you when I get settled in"—he went back home and packed his own bag.

It was after nine. He had only once in all these years been late for work: It was the morning after a blizzard. He called Bela and asked for Vander's extension. "I'll be in in an hour or so, Bob, a family crisis . . . I know the *Beacon*'s got to be put to bed."

Vander laughed. "And here we all were thinking something awful had happened to you, like for instance a meat cleaver. Nobody's talking about anything else. You're the topic of the hour."

On impulse, Timmons said, "Switch me to Kalish, will you?"

It would be all right; Kalish never answered his own phone. If Rosalie was away from her desk, Brent's secretary would pick it up.

Rosalie's voice. "Sorry, Mr. Timmons, he's in Tuesday Conference and that usually lasts most of the day, no calls allowed except if his house is on fire or his wife dropped over dead."

So Kalish hadn't fled. He made himself back up and look at it objectively. It was Ronald Kalish's word against that of

Lester Timmons, who had recently shown some unexpected sides of a character considered worthy. Could you believe it? Good old Les, whoring around and drunk out of his mind and gulping down porn like it was going out of style, sixty dollars worth of it they say . . .

Even if Kalish himself had nothing to do with Saturday's incidents, word of them was probably all over Bela now. Mrs. Leary's brother-in-law worked in Hair Products, and Madge Hingham's sister was a switchboard operator.

Thinking about this, Timmons felt a fiery blush sweep over his face. But yes, revenge, spite, malice, you had to expect it when you shouldered a heavy responsibility; when you suddenly became a man of extreme importance to a great many people. I have to expect it. I *will* cope. Just you wait and see.

He began coping by borrowing a paisley-patterned scarf of Lara's and tying it high under his chin. With this he wore a white shirt open at the neck. The bruises were completely covered and he thought the effect was unexpectedly dashing. People dressed all sorts of ways these days. Why had he always followed the out-dated rules so carefully, so willingly?

After locking up the house, he went to the Goodwood National Bank and withdrew from his and Lara's joint savings account three hundred dollars. In his car, he made two little piles of the tens and twenties and put them under the innersoles of his shoes; his own body heat ought to paste the innersoles down again.

Who would say they wouldn't like to be in my shoes, Timmons asked himself a little hysterically, as he started the car. With $150 in each of them, acting as very expensive arch cushions. He would probably need only a fraction of the money; the rest could be put back in a day or so.

He drove to the lost-looking little town of Cobb's Manor, well north of Goodwood, and checked into the Bluebird Motel, signing the register with his father's first name and his mother's maiden name: Clement Hoade. He was handed a key, went out of the office and along asphalt—soft in the heat

—to 10A. He let himself in to a featureless room which smelled rankly of cigar smoke, turned on the air conditioner to get rid of it, unpacked his bag, and in a kind of dream ("Now I'm a man without a country," he told himself) drove the eleven miles to work.

SEVENTEEN

Tuesday Conference at Bela Building Number One met fifty-two weeks a year, but any given man or woman had only one meeting a month. Everyone making $30,000 a year or over was expected to attend it. An elaborate scroll given to members at its launching five years ago had set forth its purpose: A symbiotic totaling of parts into the far-larger corporate sum. A sharing of strategies, problem-solving techniques, personnel behaviorism, new product concepts. A challenging review for each and every one of us. What are we doing and how well are we doing it—an audience of our peers is the best measure of this.

There were occasional guest speakers. A noted psychiatrist—three hours of him. An expert on the creative use of away-from-office time. A psychologist, on body motion and what it reveals about you. A speech therapist conducting oral exercises for the fuller, rounder executive voice.

A lot of people dreaded Tuesday Conference. There could be no dash, in the middle of it, for a merry lunch; this meal was eaten in the company cafeteria, and the time allotted was forty-five minutes.

One desperate executive, coming back from the men's room to one of the huge conference rooms after lunch, sat on the bottle in his back pocket and broke it.

Before opening the morning session, Charles Hines, second in command at Bela-Goodwood, addressed Brent, sitting in the third row in the theater. They were to see a film of an open-heart examination.

"What's all this about Security coming over from the Home

Office? Someone of yours, named Timmons, seems to be concerned in it. My wife heard it from our cook, of all people."

Brent had been waiting for this. "I've never noticed anything out of line about him, but from the fanfaronade he sent them—complaints and so on—they seem to think he's a bit of a nut. Just a safety check, I would assume. I'm told their real business is in Dallas."

"Oh. Good. We don't want any black marks on our end of the operation, do we."

In the cafeteria, over their veal ragout, Brent said furiously to Kalish, "You've got to do something about Timmons."

"I have," Kalish said. "Three members of the staff have gotten blackmail notes from him, and came to me with them. He says he'll be quiet if they'll pay. Not large sums but—"

"*Really?*" Brent asked, searching the other man's face.

"Really," Kalish said blandly. "Before they get to talk to him, I'll have a little chat with them. I mean, blackmail's the natural by-product for a man who's been poking and prying around trying to find out things to complain about. I suppose anyone would be tempted. But I should think it would undermine his credibility."

"I should think it would get him fired on the spot. If it can be proved," Brent said, a little uncertainly.

"I wouldn't worry about that. There are other things against him. This morning I was told that last night he knocked his wife out and she had to be taken to the hospital."

"Oh," Brent said. "Good."

"After a spirited contest between the women's basketball teams, the Belas and the Alebs, the Belas leaped (and you can take that literally) to victory. Final score was 122–98. Star on the Belas, Joanne Wolfe, made 11 baskets out of 15 shots. Congratulations to the winners and the spunky losers."

Timmons' usually nimble fingers felt heavy, clumsy, and he kept making typing errors.

"Punch flowed and presents piled up at an after-hours

kitchen shower in the Red Conference Room, Bela Building Number Three, for Kathleen Foley, who on September 1 will become the bride of Anson Young. If you don't know Kathie, you know her voice, she's one of our cheeriest switchboard gals. As for her husband-to-be, you've probably filled up many a tank with his gas—that nice bright red-and-white station on Goodwood Boulevard at Lakewood Lane."

Joe Beadon walked past the busy typewriter and grinned at Timmons' scarf. "On your way to a golf tournament or going yachting or something, Les?"

"Bad throat," Timmons explained huskily. "The air conditioning is on too high, this is my second cold this summer."

"Someone said your wife tried to strangle you last night," Beadon said. "You know the crazy scuttlebutt around here." Intrusively, no longer grinning, he looked over Timmons' shoulder at the sheet of yellow paper in his typewriter. "Are you going to put yourself into the *Beacon*? Private Eye Timmons? Sees all, knows all?" His chunky body was close, a threat.

"No," Timmons said. And, "If you don't mind, I'm busy." Must remember never again to begin a sentence with, if you don't mind. He was the man who had a lot of people like Joe Beadon on the run. He was the victor, not the victim.

And he had survived attempted murder. He was alive, and for the moment perfectly safe. People all around him. Oliver not ten feet away, deep in work at his board.

When Timmons had come in shortly after 10:30 Oliver had smiled pleasantly from his cubicle and lifted a greeting hand, as though last night's curt snub had never happened.

He had heard the racing rumors from Veronica. She had come a little shyly to his door and said, "Can I have coffee with you, Oliver? For some reason, I'm kind of sacred . . . I don't know why . . ."

What people were saying was: Timmons' wife found him in bed with a girl and the girl ran away and Timmons knocked his wife down, almost killed her, she had to have a doctor and was later taken to the hospital. Another version was that Timmons had taken up with a boardwalk prostitute in his wife's absence, and the girl attacked Timmons in a struggle to get at his wallet and his wife walked in and saved his life. Also, Timmons had been found drunk on the boardwalk on Saturday, out cold. Also, he collected dirty literature and had left a box full of the stuff lying around on his porch, and ten-year-old kids were reading it.

Oliver was appalled at the pattern he thought he was seeing. But of course, in a way inevitable, he thought. Discredit the man, shame him, undress him, ruin him, so that anything he had to say to the authorities about anybody would mean absolutely nothing.

Quietly, he asked Veronica, "And do you believe any or all of that?"

She hesitated. "Well, it's sort of out of character. But you never know. I mean, even ministers murder their wives, one did on the radio this morning. Sometimes people who *look* as if they wouldn't harm a fly . . . oh God, there he comes. That *scarf* . . . I can't stand it, I'm going over to the library and look up vitamin therapy for rheumatism, I need to anyway, I can't make head or tail of R and D's notes."

Mabel Kovarski passed Timmons' desk while he was typing a paragraph about the new baby son born to Mrs. Weldon of Accounting and Billing. "Mother and child are blooming, the fledgling Weldon bears the name of Michael, after his father."

Oliver had looked up from his board for a moment and Mabel's eyes puzzled him. Lioness' eyes, slitted down at Timmons.

She came into his cubicle and said, "I have the copy for the Ar-X bottle, and I wonder if it's going to fit in, even in small print. Will you measure it?"

She stood, very tall and straight, over the board, while he gauged the bottle copy. Something suddenly happened to his breath, and his stomach muscles tightened painfully.

He was back in the closet at Lou's house.

The smell of carnations, crisp and sweet, stingingly sweet. Forever, now recalled, to be associated with the terror of his brain going elsewhere, leaving him behind, among the legs of his trousers.

"What's the matter, Oliver?" Mabel asked sharply.

Clear-eyed, he looked up into her face. "I think I'm allergic to carnations," he said. "Not that I mean to be rude—what is it, Norell?"

"I usually wear Replique, but it was my birthday yesterday and I got this bottle and opened it this morning . . . yes, Norell. What a nose you have, Oliver."

After another minute, Oliver said, "Your copy is two lines too long. Do you think you can cut it?"

"There's nothing that can't be cut," she said, "in one way or the other. And I'm sorry I upset your stomach, Oliver, or whatever I did to you."

He had to get out of this space, this scent. He went to the water cooler and drank two cups and looked out of the window at the heavy sky. A rattle of rain abruptly hit the panes.

I should ask poor blasted undressed Timmons out to lunch, he thought. But no, that's out, don't attach yourself to a target possibly being sighted by distant guns.

For some reason he found himself thinking of another atmosphere, where the wet world outside only made shelter more pleasant. The white-brick fireplace and the painting of the children under the lilacs, the winking old glass in the corner cabinet, and the blue-eyed girl . . .

Shake off the clinging smell, the eerie whiff of danger.

"Your Timmons stopped around wanting to see you and left this message which sounds to me a bit apocalyptic . . ."

It struck him that there was only one place to be, this Tuesday in the rain, and that he should have been there long ago.

Lou started out by cursing the rain and then decided it was something of a blessing. There was no compulsion to be hearty and healthy, to swim, to treat her lungs to the immaculate air off the ocean. It was wickedly gratifying to be lolling on the sofa, reading, or trying to, while the rest of the world was at work.

"Good night, Lou darling." Maybe he used the word with *all* the women he knew, but she had never heard it sent in her direction before. Ridiculous to cherish crumbs like this; she had never done it, never had to do it, until now. Darling. From contained understated Oliver.

She heard but didn't see a car come into the drive. Wanting her peace and aloneness and being deep in Oliver instead of her book, she sat up, braced. The porch door opened and there was a light knock at the kitchen door.

Civilized people called you before driving up to your house and knocking. Preparing herself to deal briskly with some minor nuisance, she opened the door.

There was an astonishing sensation of her stomach dropping away. She summoned her breath and said, "Hello, Oliver."

"You sound winded, did I bring you running from some remote corner of your establishment?" He was smiling and his hazel eyes had an odd sparkle.

"Your dentist again? And how did you—whose car is that you came in?" Stop babbling.

"There's a pool of cars for company use on necessary business. And no, thank God, not the dentist. Am I to come in or not?"

He couldn't, possibly, be dropping by to see whether she was roaming his apartment again. That seemed a long way back, that blushing morning.

"By my watch, it's time for a drink," he said. "Especially in this weather."

There must be a point and purpose to all this, people didn't just walk out of their daily lives and characters for no reason at all. Maybe a smooth, friendly way of telling her that he had to give up the apartment? Was being transferred to another Bela office? Or that—good God!—he was going to marry the red-haired girl and they'd need larger quarters? She hadn't seen the girl in weeks, but that didn't mean he hadn't.

But you couldn't very well say, What on earth are you *doing* here.

"Necessary business being a martini?" Her voice was light and successfully merry.

"As a matter of fact, I got to thinking about you and worrying about things, and it seemed a good idea to come home and check you." He got out a tray of ice cubes. "All hell is in process of breaking loose at the office. This sounds like the advice you give to your children, but don't let anyone, any stranger, in here, Lou."

"But . . . as you said, I don't know anything about any of it, the Timmons business . . ."

"You know me," Oliver said, "which might turn out to have its drawbacks." He carried their glasses to the coffee table and put them carefully down and took off his hopsacking jacket. She was standing, hesitantly, a pace away from him, not knowing what to do with her hands or her feet or her face.

He moved quietly to her and put his arms around her and began kissing her, lightly at first. He murmured against her mouth, "My sweet Lou . . ." and then their mutual storm broke. After a famine, Lou thought hazily, a feast, a lovely, lovely feast.

Freeing her mouth for a moment, she said into his throat, "And to hell with the north-lighted studio room . . ."

"*What!*" He pulled back a little, studying her face.

". . . and the oak-plank floors and the front porch steps and the brick walk and the Teddy bear tree—"

Holding her tightly, he burst out laughing, and she followed, ripples of laughter running over their close bodies.

"Let's sit down, I'm giving at the knees," she said. "And have been ever since I opened the door."

She had never seen his face like this, radiant. He handed her her glass and said, "I'll allow you two sips before we resume. I told you that day—it was raining then, too—that I thought you were walking around inside my head."

"I couldn't help thinking it was either me or two-twenty-two, and the house had the lead. You may not be aware of it when you're sending electric charges at me . . . but I sort of knew there was *something* . . ."

"Something is hardly the word for it." Oliver looked at his glass as if he wondered what was in it, drank the contents, and reached out a brown hand.

"Come along, Lou darling."

"Come along where?" Bemused but obedient.

"To where I heard you once, waking up to me. Only then, I was on the porch. Outside."

EIGHTEEN

Timmons forced himself to stay at his desk until exactly five o'clock.

The comfort of numbers, of being surrounded with people, was counterbalanced by the aggression in the air, so sharp he could almost taste it. People had begun talking again, after lunch, but nobody talked to him; it was as if he wasn't there. He missed Veronica's pretty hair and straight back at the desk in front of his. He knew she was in; he had seen her dashing for the elevator when he had come in this morning, and uncharacteristically she hadn't even said hello.

The afternoon mail contained a mimeographed notice from Brent. Straight-faced, it said: "TO ALL. Several visitors from Bela Court will be arriving here tomorrow, Wednesday. They may very probably want to tour our department and perhaps exchange ideas with our people. Let's not, anyone, have a sore throat or an uncle's funeral to attend. Let's, except for those on vacation, make a 100% showing."

Where, Timmons wondered, had Oliver gone? Even an aloof Oliver, nearby, would have been comforting this afternoon. No cubicle ever looked as empty as his, when he wasn't in it. Rolling down his shirt sleeves and buttoning the cuffs, Timmons peered through the glass and saw on his board a sheaf of designs for the new toothpaste box. His taboret top was a litter of brushes and felt-tipped pens, the china palette brilliantly unwashed; not like tidy Oliver.

Just as the doors of his already crowded elevator were closing, a hand knifed in from the corridor to interrupt the doors' action. Three big men jammed themselves in, crushing Timmons into someone's capacious bosom. "Honest to *God!*" rose a voice out of the bosom. "*Some* people have no consideration!"

The men were Corleone, Beadon and Horner. Short as the descent to the lobby was, Timmons smelled what seemed like an ocean of drink. They'd come back in a body, he had noticed, very late from lunch, it must have been after three.

His flagging spirits picked up again. They're afraid of me. Getting up Dutch courage to face tomorrow. All because of me.

The rain made the jammed parking lot even more irritating than usual to maneuver. Car horns shouted in impatience and rage at each other. Timmons almost started to turn right at the gate and then remembered he wasn't going home, he was going to the Bluebird Motel.

He had forgotten, late for work as he was, almost murdered as he was, to check whether the Bluebird had a dining room. If they didn't, there'd be a MacDonald's or something nearby, although come to think of it, he wanted a drink too, before his dinner, a civilized gentlemanly drink.

And after dinner, he told himself, sketching a secure and orderly evening, he would come back, stretch out on the big double bed, and watch TV. Maybe stop on the way back to the Bluebird, pick up some cold milk and cookies to have while he watched.

Like a king pro tem, he was followed by an entourage, along State Highway 37.

A Pontiac, a Buick, a Ford and, several cars behind the three, an old black Dodge having its first outing in six months.

Perhaps it was the rain that made the Bluebird look shabby, second-rate. Not a particularly pleasant place to come home to, after the lonely day at Bela.

He got his key from the desk and went out into the rain again and along a row of doors to 10A. It was while he was turning the key, holding his umbrella in the other hand, tilted low to the east against the force of the rain and wind, that he became aware of his companions. Three of them.

His hand dropped from the key and he jerked around, stunned.

"It's okay, Les," Corleone said. "Get that door unlocked. You're the only one with an umbrella." He wore a large amiable grin.

"But you can't—but this is my own—"

They had moved to form a close ring around him. They were all taller than he was. An arm, Horner's, reached past him, his hand turned the key and thrust the door open.

"Okay, that is, if you keep nice and quiet," Horner said. "This is for your own good, buddy, believe me."

He closed the door and leaned against it. Corleone took the telephone receiver off its base and tossed it under the bed.

"You won't need that in here." Beadon took his umbrella and propped it in a corner.

"Got a bottle around? You look a little frail," he added, grinning.

Timmons was motionless with fear. The sheer power of flesh and muscle and bone seemed to fill the room to bursting. Menace was implicit in the way they were standing, braced, ready.

What if he shouted, screamed?

"One peep out of you and it's just too bad," Corleone said, seeing the involuntary twitch of Timmons' mouth. "Can you imagine how you'd feel—and look—after the three of us got through with you?"

"But . . . what do you *want?*"

Corleone reached into his raincoat pocket and took out an elaborate Swiss army knife and with a flick opened one of the blades, about six inches long. He stood contemplating the knife and then said, "When did you check in?"

Timmons too looked at the knife.

"This morning."

"Then you're checking out. Who's got the key? We'll pay for you and you can pay us back."

There was a movement behind Timmons. His arms were pinioned to his sides by Horner in a hard close embrace. There was a rushing rainy noise as Beadon opened the door and went out.

"Pack," Horner ordered.

Timmons went to the closet, took his suitcase off the shelf, and numbly began repacking his three-day wardrobe. One suit, two changes of underwear, two pairs of socks, two shirts, one tie, toilet articles. Had he forgotten anything? His mind wasn't working. Was he leaving something behind him here, something essential?

"Now, here it is," Horner said. "Nobody'll lay a finger on you if you do as you're told. First"—he beckoned Timmons over to the writing desk and unfolded a sheet of plain white paper—"sign your name here, about two thirds of the way down."

"Why?" Where had the rest of his voice gone, leaving only this thin rasping sound?

"It'll be on Vander's desk tomorrow morning. A signed note from you, the rest of it typed. You're sorry you caused all this trouble, and you can't face the examiners. You made it all up because you got mad that you weren't promoted. Something like that. Anyway, you cut and ran. And hid."

A posse, Timmons was thinking frantically. Vigilantes. I am going to be kidnapped. I am going to be silenced. His heart felt as though, misplaced, it was beating in his throat.

"I'll show you exactly where we want you to sign," Corleone said, using the tip of the knife blade to do so. He held it an inch away from Timmons' wrist, handing him a ball-point pen. For a second Timmons had a wild idea of writing his signature in a way that would look false, faked, but his nerve failed him. After all these years they'd know his handwriting, and the knife was so very close—

"Good boy. Now, we're taking you to a nice safe place where nobody can get at you, rip your guts out for what you've been up to," Horner said. "You'll stay there until your bloody detectives go back to Bela Court."

"But what if I—" Timmons' voice was hardly above a whisper and he couldn't make himself finish the question.

"Talk about it afterward? You won't. Not if you get it through your head you're getting your life in exchange for keeping your mouth shut," Corleone said, hard and cheerful, listening to and obviously enjoying the sound of his own dramatics. "And your wife's life. And when we get where we're going you'll sit down and write a nice thank-you note for us letting you borrow the place to hide in."

Horner, restless, wanted the floor. "We're pals of yours, see? We're helping you out of a messy situation. It'll all blow over before you know it, in a week or so everybody will be talking about something else, like is or isn't Eggena still sleeping with Ives? You'll get canned, of course, after this, but there are always other jobs."

Beadon came back. "Twenty-one-fifty for this dump," he complained, "and the carpet all spotted like that!"

He saw Timmons sway a little as his knees turned liquid under him. Almost kindly, he said, "Nothing to it. You'll come with me, and we'll have Ralph in the back just to keep things friendly. Let's have your keys, Charlie will drive your car. Can't leave it behind now that you're checked out." As though Timmons wasn't present, he said to the others, "Have to park both your cars in the lot up the street, I'll do that now."

As he turned to go out, he said, "Let the poor bastard sit down before he falls down . . ."

Timmons found himself powerfully urged to a chair and sagged into it. The knife blade in the rainy light . . . it had become the focus of his world. He hadn't said anything awful about Corleone, only that his singing arias in the men's room distracted people from their work.

His captors fell silent. Horner began to whistle under his breath. Timmons felt his eyes stinging with hot tears and reached for his handkerchief; the knife moved closer.

"Can someone hand me a tissue from the box beside the bed?" he asked. "My nose is—"

The tissue was handed. He blew his nose and wiped his eyes. Try to think. Were they acting for Carl Ives, and on his orders? He knew they played poker with Ives every Friday night. Or, for Kalish? Taking him to some place where Kalish could get at him uninterrupted? Or were they going to—dispose of him themselves, one way or another. There was a terrible air of enjoyment, relish, about them, pranksters finally letting themselves go. Several winks were exchanged over his head.

At the triple rap of knuckles on the door, Timmons was pulled up from his chair and placed between two stalwart bodies.

"You just come quietly, like they say," Horner directed. "Hang onto my arm like you've had one too many, and I'm helping you to the car."

Timmons stood motionless.

"I said, hang onto my arm," the close lips shocking his ear. Timmons obeyed, and without any simulation at all went on unsteady feet with his escorts, out the door and across the asphalt to Beadon's Pontiac, where the right-hand front door was opened for him and he was half helped, half pushed in.

His sense of unreality increased. People around, ordinary people. People going in and out of the laundromat and the ShopRite across the street, people in other cars, and he was being stolen right in their midst. His throat convulsed on a stopped scream and Horner, hearing the choking sound, leaned forward and laid heavy hands on his shoulders. "Quiet there, little fella. Charlie loaned me his knife."

Lara. Lara wouldn't expect to hear from him until tomorrow, and he had told her when he called this morning that he probably would be very, very busy so don't worry if she didn't hear from him until quite late—

And what could or would she do anyway? Notify the police? And have real or imagined scandals dumped on her head, on her husband, on her home? And, oh God, if and when, not hearing from him, she did call, she'd be told about the note saying that he had run away and hidden.

Ferdinand Lane (Laney to his friends and lovers) went into the phone booth at the corner of the Bluebird's parking lot, where he could keep his eye on the door of 10A. He had been following Timmons since the morning trip to the hospital.

He was in his early twenties, a mysterious blend of nationalities. He had slanting dark eyes, a full rosy mirthful mouth, dust-colored skin, a markedly wide-nostriled nose, and hair dyed a bright orange-blond and worn in an ear-covering cap of curls. He was small and slight but wirily powerful. He was available for a number of tasks if well paid for them. The job didn't matter as long as you got on, got by, got away with it.

When the phone at the other end was picked up, he said, "He was followed from Bela here to the Bluebird by three cars. When they got here, three guys—they work there, I saw them come out—moved up on him, hustled him through the door." Appreciatively, "It didn't look like he was going to have too good of a time inside."

"Keep on it," Kalish said. "But remember, don't do anything rash, dear boy, where *you* can be seen doing it."

"There's another thing. There's an old black beat-up car with a woman in it. She came out behind them from the Bela lot, and from then on she kept two cars between her and their three. She's parked a little way up a side street just beyond the lot. She keeps twisting her head around, watching the Bluebird and their cars."

"What does she look like?"

"Hard to tell in this light, at this distance, dark glasses, scarf tied around her head, no chick."

Kalish laughed. "The way things are shaping up, it looks as though someone else may do our dirty work for us. If they do—efficiently—your time won't be wasted, we'll settle for half."

Ten minutes later, "They're taking him to one of their cars. He's kind of dragging his heels. No marks on him. Yet, or that I can see. The woman's still across the street."

"Well, to horse and away, and do stay close to the party, dear boy."

Laney got into his battered little dark green van which proclaimed on both sides, "Acme Dry Cleaners" and waited.

He had found to his gratification that people seldom noticed or remembered dry cleaners' vans.

Traffic on Route 142 was heavy in spots. Tractor-trailers loomed out of the windy wet purple gloom. A signpost told Timmons which direction they were going. Philadelphia, 52 miles. They were going west.

He had stopped thinking, and for a while, traveling an unfamiliar crisscrossing of streets and roads before coming to the main highway, had concentrated on trying to stop the shaming involuntary shaking of his facial muscles and head and hands.

"Have a cigarette," Beadon said, pushing an opened pack across the seat. "No messing around with the dashboard lighter, though." He placed a firm hand over it.

A cigarette suddenly sounded to Timmons like the most wonderful thing in the world. If he could manage to get it lit, and to hold it between his trembling fingers.

More shame, his fumblings. But he finally did manage. He could turn and press the lighted tip into Beadon's cheek. But that would only wreck the car and might kill all three of them. To underline this possibility, another tractor-trailer came roaring down the hill on the other side.

"Rotten old road. They need a new one," Horner said. "But we've only got another half mile or so—"

A gap in the traffic allowed Beadon to make a left turn across the eastbound lane. In a few moments they were in a muffle of silence, headlights showing wet green scrub pines on either side of the narrow twisting macadam road.

Timmons thought he knew what it was they were heading into. Some portion of the New Jersey pine barrens, known to locals as the Piney Woods. He had a few scraps of information about the barrens. That they were state-owned, that there was a battle on and off to build an immense jet airport in the midst of their near-virgin wilderness. That the streams were pure and sand-bottomed, and that you could go a mile through the pines, in the most densely populated state in the country, without encountering another human being.

To keep the Pontiac and the Ford in sight, Mabel Kovarski twice risked her life, passing a gasoline tank truck in spite of the solid yellow center stripe forbidding this, and later a doddering garbage truck. But it no longer seemed to matter very much, these brushes with violent death.

When she turned left, across the traffic, braked rubber screamed dangerously close, but miraculously, she made it again. As though, with a mission of such vital importance, nothing could harm her until it was accomplished.

She was grateful for the dry cleaner's van forty feet or so ahead of her. Impersonal, commercial, a faceless kind of vehicle. If they looked back, that's what they'd see, nothing to give them any concern. The van had passed her a few minutes before the turnoff.

She now couldn't see her quarry, but so far there had been no openings in the woods on either side, and they couldn't be going much faster than she was on the curving pot-holed road. On an unexpectedly straight stretch, they reassuringly appeared, turning right, headlights raking the lower branches of the pines.

The van turned right, too. Bless that van. A sandy dirt track, grassy in the middle, only a car-width wide. She drove very slowly, now, then stopped and switched off her lights. Well up ahead, the Pontiac and the Ford had pulled off the road and stopped on a rough sandy patch in front of a cabin. The van passed by and disappeared.

Lights went out in the two cars. Doors were opened and slammed. A flashlight beam shot toward the wooden porch steps of the cabin. If they turned it in the direction of her car—

She fingered her leather shoulder bag. It held the Beretta her father had brought back from his service in Italy during the Second World War. Nervous about burglars, he had shown her how to load it, years ago, and explained the firing mechanism to her. It was kept in a Maxwell House coffee can in the umbrella stand just inside the front door.

The flashlight, intent on its own business, did not turn her way.

NINETEEN

Timmons' legs could barely support him when he got out of the car. He wanted to let himself fall, faint, be out of this forever, one way or another.

Strong urging arms got him up the porch steps. The window-shades were down but thin cracks of light showed around the edges.

"Good old Whit," Horner said. "Right on time."

The door was opened to them by a tall cadaverous man in his seventies with protuberant dark eyes and scant hair dyed black, looking painted onto his high skull. He wore battered army fatigues and held an opened can of beer.

"Greetings, General MacArthur," Beadon said. "I could have sworn you'd passed on."

Horner's great-uncle Whit had been, until he retired, a warder at Holmsburg Prison.

Horner led Timmons across the room to a straightbacked chair at a square wooden table. "Sit down, make yourself at home," he said. "Welcome to our fishing and hunting lodge. Not too fancy, but it's comfortable."

Timmons' eyes swept what might or might not be his place of execution. The cabin was obviously a one-room affair. Four blanketed bunks on two walls, an old couch with a torn cover, two castoff-looking chairs, a galleylike kitchen arrangement in one corner. Bare dirty wood floor, a dozen hooks hung with weekend garments, fishing poles propped between them, a row of leather and rubber boots under them. A smell of sweat and damp wood and cigar smoke. An unshaded light bulb hanging from the ceiling. A back door not far from the table where he sat.

With a thud of the heart, he saw the rifles—or were they shotguns?—in a rack beside the front door.

Whit took one of these weapons down and stroked the butt with a gnarled hand.

"Meet my Uncle Whit," Horner said. "Crack shot. Won't touch a hair of your head, though, if you behave. And by that I mean just do what you're told, and you'll be all right. You don't have to worry about keeping quiet, there're no neighbors around."

Beadon unfolded another piece of white bond paper and put it on the table, handing Timmons a pen. "I'll dictate, you write."

All of the company looked with interest at Timmons' fluttering butterfly hand.

Beadon went to a cabinet above the sink and took out a bottle. He poured brandy into a jelly glass and gave it to Timmons. "Doesn't matter if it hits you later, you aren't going anywhere."

Timmons drank it down gladly and recklessly. If you were out, gone, you wouldn't know what they were doing to you. An immediate fire was lit inside his ribcage.

"Give him three minutes," Corleone said, as if he were timing an egg. He poured three more drinks into oddly assorted glasses, and lifted his.

"To the man with fifty complaints," he said. There was a sort of throttled schoolboy laughter. Whit slapped his thigh, and almost bent double.

"*That* little fella?" he asked incredulously. "*He* was trying to get you fired?"

"Now then, Timmsy." Beadon loomed. "This is to thank—well, start writing."

Timmons wrote. "—Joe Beadon, Charlie Corleone and Ralph Horner for letting me use their fishing and hunting cabin in the barrens to hide in when the Switzerland people came over."

Beadon continued to dictate. "And here is my word and

bond that for this favor I will pay them one thousand dollars when those pinkertons have gone home."

The hand was separated from the head; it went on writing. Then Timmons said on a long sigh, "A thousand dollars—"

"Are you worth that much to you, Timmsy?" Corleone asked. "If not—"

Rain blasted the panes. Timmons stared at the shade, which had a long tear down its center, the plastic curling away to show a wet stormy inch of blackness trapped under towering trees.

"Now sign it," Beadon ordered. "Because your hands aren't going to be all that much good to you from now on."

He signed it, and was tidily roped to his chair by Whit.

I had this dream, Timmons was telling himself vaguely, his senses slipping a little. I was in this cabin, tied to a chair, and four men cooked themselves hamburgers and home fried potatoes, and pushed my chair away from the table and sat down and ate and talked and laughed and drank brandy and whiskey and beer, and all the time the rain was pouring down on the roof. And I started to feel numb, first my feet and then my hands and then my head. And then numb all over.

"Dishes'll give you something to occupy yourself with, Whit," Horner said after a timeless interval. "Sling him a burger later if he gets hungry. Your relief comes on at eight A.M. If he has to use the bathroom, untie him and go with him, you and your gun."

Sated with drink and dinner, he turned to Timmons. "Want a glass of water or something? Give him some water, Whit."

A glass of water was held to his lips and half of it went down his shirt front.

There was a yawning that spread, an air of repletion, contentment; men ready, now, to leave a party that had exhausted its pleasures for them.

"Now mind, Whit"—Horner said, shaking a finger—"you wouldn't believe it, but he's dangerous. Don't close an eye."

"This little fella, *dangerous?*" Whit laughed a scraggy laugh. "If you say so. 'Night, boys."

The door closed noisily behind them. A car engine started,

rivaled for a moment with its noise the rain, and then there was only the sound of wind and water and heaving branches in the cabin.

Was it the brandy speaking?

Timmons looked over at the old man, folded into a corner of the couch, reading a newspaper.

"I'll give *you* the thousand, if you'll let me go," he said. He hadn't thought his way to it. The words just tumbled out of his mouth.

Whit looked up from his paper with a startled and then beaming expression in his eyes.

"You would?"

"Yes."

"But you'd have to overpower me, shoot me, cut me or something," Whit said, considering. "And I'm not interested in getting hurt. Let's put our thinking caps on. That's your car out there?"

"Yes."

"But those fellows'll have the keys?"

"My wife is careless about keys," Timmons explained. "I always keep an extra set on me. Just in case."

It was nice, even for a few minutes, not to feel used and helpless and governed by terror.

Eyes narrowing in suspicion, "How do I know you'd pay me? Once you get loose you could just run to the cops."

"I'm a man of my word," Timmons said. "And you can have a hundred and fifty in cash right now, as proof of it, and an i.o.u. I'd have to go to the savings bank for the rest of it."

"Cash, you say. Well now, about your escape--But Ralphie has a rough temper when he gets going, it'd have to be good." Whit stroked his jaw tenderly as if in remembrance of a blow.

"I could have managed to knock over my chair, and when you came to pick it up I could have kicked the gun out of your hands and got hold of it–"

"Makes me look too stupid. Remind me after this beer to do your ankles."

"A friend of theirs was going by in a car," invented Timmons eagerly, "and saw the lights and knew they weren't usually there in the middle of the week. He suspected burglary and banged on the door. You had untied me to go to the bathroom and I just dashed out—"

"Sometimes they drink and play cards out here, any night of the week. To get away from their wives."

"I could set the place on fire—"

"If their ever-blessed camp burned down, they'd throw me onto the embers." Whit finished his beer and reached for his spool of heavy nylon twine.

"Before you do that, speaking of the bathroom, I have to—um—could you—"

"Pee?" Whit picked up his gun. "Mind your manners, this thing's loaded good. If you try to jump me, it'll go off, I promise you." He put it down again on the arm of the couch, came over, and bent to the knots behind Timmons' back.

Mabel Kovarski waited a long ten minutes after the sound of the Pontiac lost itself in the night. Had they gone to get something? Food supplies? A bottle? Would they be coming back?

She had driven her father's old black Dodge off the lane and deep into the trees, there would be no sign of it to their eyes. After that, she waited on a rise behind the house, under a pine so densely sheltering that only an occasional drop of water hit her head and shoulders.

Then, slowly, she began circling the house, keeping close to the walls. She found at the far window at the back the shade with a crack in it, and there, not four feet away from her, sat Timmons, tied to a chair.

Her hand flipped open the shoulder-bag and closed on the Beretta. How cold the metal was.

She saw again through his eyes, watching her ripping, raging, strewing Marie Eggena's office to pieces. The unseen gaze was a violation she found unbearable. Yes, Mabel Annette Kovarski, unemployable, mad, as witnessed . . . Their only income was her father's Social Security and her salary. And she couldn't erase it all, change her name, run away, be someone else. Because there he was, nine tenths of the time in his wheelchair. And no power on earth could pry him from the cocoon, the house he had patiently come to own, the house he had brought his young wife, Annette, to.

There was a movement in the shadows and another man appeared close to the crack, bending behind Timmons, doing something.

She waited. The ropes fell away and Timmons got up unsteadily and began chafing his hands together. The other man stepped back and away from him.

The brain, the simplest--and he was so close. Her right hand, holding the gun, was trembling a little. She gave it a cushioning brace with her left hand. Aiming for Timmons' head, she shot off the lobe of his right ear. Unaware of it until seconds later, when the echoes hit her, she screamed as she fired.

The back door crashed open and in the light pouring from it she saw the old man with his gun plunging out. She stood frozen, and then began to run from him, into the trees. She tripped on an exposed root and, cursing, he stumbled and fell heavily over her, pinning her to the ground. His gun went off thunderously.

There was, curiously, no pain, just shock and blood. Timmons stood in a paralysis looking at the impossible idea of freedom. Not out the back way, not after that second shot. Or was it really only one, and did it just keep reverberating? He walked slowly to the front door, opened it, and then ran down the stairs and over to his car. He wasn't clear in his head whether he was fleeing from something. Or to something.

TWENTY

Laney found himself diverted as well as puzzled by the evening's proceedings. He had hidden the van around a curve in the sand track beyond the house and slipped up onto Mabel's rise. He wasn't ten feet from her when he heard a small cough. He couldn't see her and, pressing against a tree trunk, was equally sure she couldn't see him. Couldn't have heard him, either, the soft wet swaying of the pine boughs would have blurred out the light sure-footed record of his passage through the trees.

The woman in the beat-up black car, who had risked her neck to keep up with them, and then had followed his van into the barrens. Waiting, alone. Obviously not a member of the party. Obviously up to no good.

Laney always felt entertained when in the presence of other people involved in wrongdoing. Those three big slobs, she hadn't a prayer. But hell, let her try.

". . . it looks as though someone else may do our dirty work for us . . ."

Mentally, he prepared a report for Kalish just to keep the sequence straight in his memory. The slobs drove off, back toward the highway. Timmons wasn't with them, he'd been left behind in the cabin, and Laney figured he wasn't alone. After taking all this trouble, they wouldn't want to have to worry about his finding a way to get loose, get out.

He understood the woman's long silent wait; afraid they might be planning to come back. He watched as she finally moved down the rise and close to the house. She would have been invisible except for the slivers of light escaping here and there from the edges of the shades, flicking her before she disappeared again.

She was at the back of the cabin, now, having completed her circling. What was she going to do? If she was going to do anything at all, if she wasn't just plain crazy—

Her driving, and her stillness under her tree, and her waiting, all seemed a little crazy to him. Maybe she was a girl friend and had some crazy Girl Scout idea of rescuing him.

The sound of the shot brought a deep gasp from him. The back door was flung open and an old coot with a gun came rushing out, and the woman ran from him, and the two of them went crashing down. While the woman struggled with the shouting, cursing man, Timmons came running out of the front door of the house and down the steps with, Laney thought, as much style as if he had one wooden leg. Staggering, holding onto his ear. *He'd* been shot at, then, maybe it was all over, all done?

No, he was getting into his car. Starting his car. Turning his car around.

From the old man's furious shouting, Laney gathered that his prey was slipping through the woods parallel with the sand track but well back from it. He had no more time, however, with which to record the chase. He ran for his van and resumed his own mission, his own chase.

He had to stop a minute or two where the macadam road met the highway, for an opening in the traffic, but Timmons' car had to stop too.

Entering the eastbound lane, he saw the old Dodge pull to a halt, waiting its turn. Although a crazy woman like that, shooting through drawn window shades—at who? The old coot or Timmons?—wouldn't wait long.

Kalish, Timmons thought. Kalish. Kalish. Kalish is somewhere behind me. He got them to put me away in a safe lonely place where this time, nobody could stop him. Nobody except Whit, and Whit was in with them. They'd fix it so it looked as though I killed myself, or something.

His heart was making such a thunder in his chest that he was afraid it would kill him, right there behind the wheel. It had had too much to take, his heart had.

If he just thought about his driving, and the wet and perhaps slippery road, and nothing else, nothing else at all—

What did Kalish's car look like? Yes, big, dark gold color, but he didn't know what make it was. He looked into the driving mirror but colors disappeared between the mercury vapor lamps. Was that a dark gold car behind the immediately following vehicle, a van of some kind?

The reflected sight of his blood-smeared cheek and neck horrified him. He felt for his earlobe and found it wasn't there and was immediately gripped by nausea. His car slowed for a moment and the van braked savagely.

Have to be careful. Couldn't faint, at 55 miles an hour. It wouldn't do to die in a rubble of metal after he had gotten away from Kalish, not just once, but twice.

He suddenly remembered the split in the window shade. So that was why he had been placed by the table, bundled and roped. A neat, close and immobile target for Kalish, to pick off at his leisure.

To the right, he saw and recognized a lighted garden furniture store that had barely registered on his terrified gaze on the way out, on the way to the cabin. He must be, he calculated, about halfway to Goodwood. But where was he heading?

Not home, home was dangerous, impossible, a yawning trap, a deathly place. Not the Bluebird, his room had been canceled and anyway they knew about the Bluebird, they might have been notified by Whit and be waiting for him there, those three men—

He could try to find another motel room in the ring of towns around Goodwood, but now in August, Labor Day approaching, they would probably be jammed. And if he did find a room, he would be alone, unprotected . . .

Of course Whit would have called at the very least Ralph. Ralphie, who had such a rough temper when he let it go.

They would be out looking for Lester Timmons, fleeing back to where his life was centered.

He felt in his bones a certainty that someone must be following him. They'd worked so hard and risked so much, Kalish and the poker players.

Run to Lara and her mother? Too long a drive, too many things could happen on the way, and he might bring, on his heels, some sort of disaster to them.

". . . and your wife's life."

The police. He had no idea where the Goodwood police station was. Finding it would entail stopping the car at a telephone booth, looking up the number, standing lighted and vulnerable. There were no pedestrians to stop and shout at, ask for directions, on these rainy roads with few houses, roads given over to commerce.

And if he did deliver himself up to the police—

Yes, officer, almost strangled last night and shot at tonight. You can see the wound in my ear, or rather that part of it isn't there—could you possibly put me in a cell here tonight for safety?

Oh God no, the Bela security people tomorrow, and heralding his own entrance the fact that he had just spent a night in jail. Suit wrinkled. Unshaven.

But of course they wouldn't let him spend the night there anyway. It's against regulations, he would be told. Why don't you just—soothing voices—go on home, Mr. Timmons, and the patrol car will check your house every half hour or so.

It was a little after 9:30 now. He had to stay alive for another twelve hours, and then there wouldn't be any point, any more, in killing him. He'd be at his desk at Bela. Impossibly having survived and ready to answer any and all inquiries put to him.

He had almost forgotten, over the distressing hours, the *point* of all this. His hour. His day. His victory over everything that had happened to him. At home and at Bela.

But the real point, a small inner voice said, was to stay alive through the night. Just to *be* alive from then on.

There was only one place to go. There was only one safe place and one safe man in the whole torn-apart world to go to.

Eyes aching, he kept checking the mirror; a double strain, having to see the haunted bloody face there. A large dark gold car passed him and his throat protested with a half-sobbing gasp.

Passing the Farms River High School, he got caught in a reassuring jam of cars leaving after some sporting or dramatic or musical event within.

Not more than a mile or so, now.

Accompanied by a trickle of cars from the high school, and the dry cleaner's van, and four cars behind it by a black Dodge, he turned into Lambert Road.

When he got to the white house on the corner, he made a left turn, passed the house's driveway, and proceeded very slowly up Jefferson Street. So close to haven, he couldn't now be reckless, careless. There was a dark house on the right, with a garage at the end of its short drive. He pulled the car up to the garage doors, switched off his lights, got out, and in the opaque purple near-blackness under the lowering pouring skies, tried the doors. Not locked. He opened them and put the car in the garage and closed the doors again behind him.

There was a street-light stanchion in the middle of the block but gulfs of darkness to either side and ahead of him. He half ran across to a stand of heavy low-branched Norway spruces and slipped into the drive of 222.

His imagination placing riflemen in the immense trees around him, and on the high porches of the great darkened house next door, he gathered his being into himself like a man dodging a hail of bullets. No lock on the winter porch door, just an instantly accommodating latch.

He stood listening, at the kitchen door. There had been some sort of light, he remembered, as he passed along the house wall. He had no idea of how the entrance to Oliver's apartment was arranged. Inside stairway? His hand, lifting itself to knock, stopped. Don't. He might, he just might even under the appalling circumstances, be ordered out by Oliver into the night, the empty crowded night.

With remembering fingers, he reached under the clay flowerport on the table to his right and found the key. Very softly and carefully, he opened the door, and recorded what was to him a sweet and absolute silence except for the rain, its noise reduced now to a homely pleasant murmur.

One lamp was on in the kitchen. He went through the doorway into the center room. There were two glasses on the coffee table, an olive left in one of them. A faint flapping sound worried him, and he went to the bedroom door and saw it was only the white curtain in the wind. The bed was softly, drowsily untidied.

He caught a faint whiff of perfume near and drew from the air another unclassifiable sort of scent, or feel, or impression, of repose, kindness, happiness. In a daze of relief, of safety, he found himself thinking, What a . . . contented house this is.

The shades were pulled down to the tops of the cafe curtains, so he couldn't be seen, standing here, snatching his share of some kind of joy, rest. But he mustn't linger; they could be back at any time. Together. Or she, alone; or Oliver, alone.

He went back to the center room and his eye caught the white telephone under the lighted lamp on a step table at the end of the sofa. Guiltily but swiftly, he bent and cut the wire with his pen-knife and pushed the cut end under the table. It wouldn't do, after all this, for Oliver to hand him over to the protection of the police. To have them take him out into the night again, take him home.

Was there another telephone in the darkened room at the front of the house? He peered in, then circled it, and saw no phone, but gazed at a door in the right-hand wall, white, tall, formal. He tried the knob and it was motionless; some kind of seal on the door. Perhaps his access to his apartment was up the back stairway he had noted in the kitchen.

Irresolute, he went back to the light, to the bowl of floating pink cosmos on the coffee table, to the peace. He had no plan, except to throw himself on Oliver's mercy for the night.

Suddenly he recalled his wrong turning in the hall, when he had come visiting here in search of Oliver, when, *yesterday?* Surely that door he had bumbled toward led to a cellar? A very decorative door, with a painting hung on it, a crowd of beach umbrellas.

He shot the bolt and saw a steep wooden stairway with a heavy exposed house beam running along horizontally beside it. Then he needn't bother them *at all*, just spend the night in the cellar, and in the morning ask if he could use the shower and Oliver's razor. People didn't have to do anything to furnaces in summertime—

Was there time for a glass of water? He was desperately thirsty. The bathroom was only a foot or so away. He snatched a clear plastic cup from beside the basin, filled it, drank, filled it again, and heard a car engine in the drive, doors slamming, a snatch of laughter. No time, now, to take care of Oliver's telephone, upstairs, but that would no longer be necessary. Or did *she* live upstairs, and was this Oliver's apartment? Or did they . . . share the house between them.

He pulled the cellar door to behind him, wedging it with a bit of folded newspaper from a pile on the shelf at his left, making sure the wedge didn't go all the way through the crack, to the other side. Then he seated himself against the comforting beam, several steps down, and tried to listen, over the anxious heavy beating of his heart.

TWENTY-ONE

Disposed comfortably on the sofa beside her, an arm around her, Oliver lifted his lips an inch from her cheek to ask with curiosity but with happy certainty, "What about that—what was his name—Larkin, here in June?"

"He got tired of my saying no, weekends—that I needed the country air." Lou laughed softly in her throat.

"And Finch. Is he married? Not that that would deter a man of his authoritarian airs—"

"Divorced."

"Eye on you for the next one?"

"Maybe. Unreciprocated."

"*He* was when I stopped running and began pursuing. Although I suspected that you were my girl from that first picnic on the porch steps."

"You didn't have to pursue very far. *I* didn't do any running to say the least."

"But Lou," mouth flickering over hers again, "why would a sensible girl like you run from her love?" After several moments, and laughing a little, "Is your apartment really being painted?"

"Yes. They asked me months ago when I'd find it most convenient."

The telephone in the apartment above started ringing, on its table almost directly over their heads. "Hell with it," Oliver said. It rang ten times, stopped, and after an interval of two or three minutes began again.

"Oh God, maybe my mother, from California? I'll go answer

it, and I have to bring down some things for tomorrow anyway–"

He got up, lithe and glowing, bent to kiss the top of her head and ran through the kitchen and out the porch door. Lou, with a hand touching her tossed hair, went smiling to the bathroom to tidy her face. And to see how it looked, in the mirror, to be loved by Oliver.

In the hall, she noticed that the painting on the cellar door was sharply crooked. She flicked it with a forefinger and the frame banged lightly against the door. There was something–just the barest breath of sound, a kind of gasp. Too surprised and puzzled to feel immediate fear, she opened the door and stood looking down into the terrified eyes of Lester Timmons, sitting a few steps down, hugging himself against unknown disaster.

"I was hiding," he said a little above a whisper. "I didn't want to trouble you."

His pallor, his look of despair and his seeming to be waiting for a kick, or a shove, made her say, "You must come out of there. Is there really–is someone after you?"

Clinging to his wooden beam as if it was a raft on an angry ocean, Timmons said, "You won't make me leave right away? Until I tell you–until I tell Oliver what–I think I heard his voice?"

"He's upstairs, he'll be right down," Lou said, as much to herself as to Timmons. She held out a hand to help him up. "Come along, Mr. Timmons."

The animal fear in the air around him caught at her pity. No human being should look like that, stripped naked of itself, of all its normal prides and protections.

Again, she said, "Come along. It's all right. I think you very badly need a drink."

In a rage of impatience, Decimus Finch shouted, "I've been trying to get Lou for hours! First no answer on her phone, just ringing, and for the last twenty minutes nothing at *all*."

"Storm knocked it out, maybe," Oliver said politely. "That does happen."

"Well, as you seem on such familiar terms with the ways of the house and its other inhabitant," Finch said caustically, "I'd appreciate it if when you track her down you'd give her a message. Nobody knows where she put the Nexus file and I must have it, absolutely, without fail, tomorrow morning. Will you have her call me?"

"Without fail," Oliver said deliberately, the words informing the other man that he knew exactly when and where the other inhabitant was to be found.

He was in the bedroom, collecting his clothes for tomorrow when the telephone rang again. It was his friend and unofficial agent in New York, Peter Gudunov, who had a dressy midtown gallery, where he sold to the rich, and a loft gallery in SoHo, where he promoted and encouraged newer talents. He had in the past year sold six of Oliver's pictures at prices the artist himself would never have dreamed of asking.

He too began with a blast. "For God's sake, do you live in an open field or something? I tried to get you at work and nobody knew where you were, all afternoon, and then there wasn't any answer here, either, for hours—and I tell you, Oliver, I'm frantic."

Peter Gudunov had a way of becoming frantic very easily and very colorfully. "For one thing, your show, the two-man show, has to be pushed up a month because—" Interminably, Peter, who spent a large portion of his day on the telephone, told him why. "And that raises a thousand questions and problems, and we've got to tackle them right *now* because otherwise I will promise you total wreckage."

Knowing what lengths the phone call literally might go to, Oliver said, "Just a minute." He went into the kitchen and poured a drink and brought it back to his chair. He was tempted to hang up, call Lou, and then call Peter back, but, a long long lovely night ahead . . . business, very possibly good business, before pleasure.

Lou had just seated Timmons in a corner of the sofa when there was a light but insistent knocking on the kitchen door.

Oh good, Oliver. The lock must have snicked itself when he went out.

She opened the door in warm eagerness, to Mabel Kovarski.

"Good evening, sorry to—" The tall woman in the dark raincoat identified herself. "May I come in a minute?"

Timmons had just raised his glass. He set it down on the coffee table and again crossed his arms tightly, protectingly, over his chest.

"Oh, Les, I'm so glad, I was so *worried* . . ." She sat down, crouchingly, in the little walnut rocker at the hearth corner, close to Timmons.

Lou stood, watching and only mildly wondering, not quite attending to the scene. She wore her floating flowered long dress and looked without knowing it shining, transported.

Office matters, no doubt. A friend of Timmons who was worried about him. Helpful, under the circumstances.

Mabel said, "I don't want to frighten you, but Veronica called me a little while ago. She's been half out of her mind about it all evening. She said she heard Ives talking to Marie Eggena, they were just around the corner from her, near the water cooler. Marie was babbling away and Ives said, 'Timmons won't be here tomorrow, I promose you that.' Veronica didn't know what to think of it, but she thought it sounded terrible and finally she called me . . ."

"Can I get you a drink, Ms. Kovarski?" Lou asked.

The golden eyes raked her and gave her an odd feeling at the back of her neck. Some kind of chill, or tingle.

Even in her preoccupation, she felt that underneath the woman's apparent concern about her fellow employee was some kind of fierce unstoppable urgency.

Timmons said nothing. He took a long pull at his drink and the wretched coughing and choking began. He recovered and wiped his eyes with his handkerchief, remembering when he had not been allowed to do himself this service in the room at the Bluebird.

Mabel had always, until a short time ago, been nice, kind, reliable— His mind hazed. Maybe he had only imagined some deep and frightening change. She wanted to help him now, didn't she? Now, on the very worst night of his life. Even worse than the night in the garage, with Lara and Rainer in his house, on his sofa.

"Anyway, Les, we have a spare room, the bed's all made up. My father's there, and I'll be there, and you won't be alone, when you leave here. No one can get at you, and you'll be all right until morning, and I'll drive us to work, you can leave your car at the house and pick it up later. That way, no chance of anyone following you."

The passion of pleading made Lou wonder if this woman was in love with him. One-track mind, she chided herself. She noted the paling of the knuckles that gripped the leather shoulder strap of her handbag. Timmons' list, she thought, was certainly coming to a boil. If the list was what this was all about, and it must be.

"Thank you, Mabel, but I don't, actually, want to leave here. I don't want to go out again. That is, if Oliver . . ." Thin faraway voice. "No, I really don't want to go out again, into the . . ." He left it unfinished.

"But *Les*—" She looked from him to Lou. "You don't want to impose on *strangers*."

"We've met, haven't we?" Timmons said, addressing Lou.

"Yes, of course." She wanted very much to go out and around the house and up the steps and get Oliver, and let him take over. He'd know about this woman. She didn't, but what she did know was that there was something very wrong about the atmosphere of the room. Phone calls, though, perhaps his mother—she knew he wasn't a man of the phone-dithering variety.

Mabel looked at her watch. "Dad will be beginning to worry, I dashed right out of the house after Veronica called—"

Laney, from behind a porch pillar at the red house next door, watched the unfolding of events. His van was pulled up at the far side of the house.

Nothing had happened for ten minutes or so after, on foot, he saw Timmons put his car in a garage, cross the street, and go in at the back porch of the white house.

Then a car turned into the drive and stopped. By the dim light from the kitchen window he saw a man and girl get out of it and go in, hand in hand.

Ten minutes more of nothing happening. A telephone ringing somewhere. The man, youngish, white pants, blue-and-white striped shirt, looking fast and fit and well able to account for himself, ran around the house and in at the front. It wasn't another minute or so until the crazy woman in the dark raincoat walked up to the porch door and went in.

Maybe she was still going to do his work for him. There was only the girl there now, and Timmons. But he was not good at waiting, and at relying on other people. Okay, just play it by ear. He went and opened the van. As always, his motorcycle was in it, and a lightning way to change his appearance: old faded-blue crew hat with a bushy blond moustache tucked in it, dirty anonymous raincoat, dark goggles in its pocket.

And on a hook to the left, his "deliveries," which often came in handy.

"It's very kind of you, Mabel, but I'd rather stay here," Timmons was repeating, and halfway through the stubborn timid refusal there was another knock.

Surely Oliver, this time.

A young man, peculiar-looking, walked into the kitchen, two garments in plastic wrappers on hangers slung on a thumb over his shoulder.

"Wow, nice and dry in here," he said, and looked past her into the warmly lighted room beyond. Mabel Kovarski, crouched on her rocker was directly in his line of vision.

He looked brightly at Lou, who had moved back to the doorway. "Mrs. Ellicott? Neither rain nor dark nor night and all that stuff, twenty-four hour service—I've got your gown and your cashmere cardigan. They were promised to you and here they are, right on the button."

Interrupting the unexplained tensions, the—yes—menaces in the room behind her, misdelivered clothes were a mundane relief.

"Sorry, you've got the wrong address, I'm not Mrs. Ellicott and those aren't my clothes."

"But they *said* this address and I've driven all the way from Neptune City," the young man with the orange-yellow hair and the pink mirthful mouth protested. "Lady had to have it before ten, I even broke the speed limit." He looked indignant. "Maybe that other lady in there—?"

"No, she doesn't live here, she just dropped in."

"Well then, can I use your phone? It's got to be around here, Lambert Road, they said, Farms River. Two-twenty-two, they said."

"Of course. In there, at the end of the sofa."

Laney walked into the room, casting an eye at Timmons drawn deeply, defensively into his cushions. He laid his plastic-covered garments on the round dining table in one corner, went to the phone and picked it up. He frowned, fiddled with the buttons on the base, replaced the receiver, and picked it up again.

To Lou, he said, "You've got a dead line. Unless"—his slanting dark eyes went to Timmons—"someone's cut it on you."

Then he straightened up and his manner changed. "Mrs. Ellicott—oh, sorry, wrong name but for me wrong job too."

He reached into his pocket and took out a gun.

Oh God, robbery, Lou thought, and Oliver on his damned phone upstairs. What a fool, to have let him in at this hour, together with this other sinister stranger—

She wanted to scream for Oliver but the gun in the thin hand kept her silent. All right, take my bag, take the Kovarski woman's, let's get it over with. He did go over to the woman on the rocking chair and held the gun lightly at her temple. "Handbag, please."

Torn, ragged face, gold eyes blazing—Lou was bolted by

her savagery. She slowly let go of the strap of her bag and Laney took it off her shoulder and tossed it behind the sofa.

"By wrong job, I mean, I'm Bela security, ma'am," again addressing Lou. "Funny, I still think of you as Mrs. Ellicott. I'm here to collect Timmons. I've been following this woman, she tried to kill him tonight. He'll be better off under guard till morning."

Timmons sat very still. He was to be collected, taken off by this boy, who was sending waves of terror through the last refuge, through the house where Oliver lived. Taken off and done away with.

He saw Laney in one light only: an instrument of death.

He managed a small "No" on a weary exhalation of breath. He was so tired, tireder than he'd ever been in his life.

Somehow getting it out, Lou said, "But if there was some kind of attempted murder–why are you here, why not the police?" Her voice kited up on the final few words.

"Complicated matter, ma'am, it will all be explained to you later. For your safety and his, I've got to get him out right now." He reached down a hand and pulled Timmons to his feet. "Come on, fella."

Timmons uttered a crying caw, the sound of a lost soul.

Oliver, Lou thought, Oliver, *Oliver*–

From the kitchen doorway, Oliver said, "Lou, what's this all about?" His voice was very quiet.

They stood arranged in their tableau. Lou, her eyes too large, holding onto the back of a slipper chair. Laney in the center of the Mahal clutching Timmons' wrist. Mabel Kovarski bent frantically into herself, on the rocker. A slither of plastic, clothes on hangers, draped over the dining table.

In a voice he had never heard before, careful and unreal, Lou said, "Mr. Timmons was hiding in the cellar because he said there was someone after him. Then Ms. Kovarski came, she said the same thing and she wanted to take him to her house for safety. Then this man came, with those clothes–" She gestured with an arm that had gone limp. "And *he's* taking Mr. Timmons away for his safety too, he says he's with

Bela security. And that she"—she couldn't see Mabel Kovarski's face and didn't want to—"tried to kill him tonight."

"Good thing I went back and called the police, upstairs, I heard peculiar noises down here, I was listening outside the kitchen door for a moment or so," Oliver lied. "In the meantime," to Laney, "you'll let me see your credentials, of course, as this man is a guest in our house."

Laney took two steps forward, dragging Timmons with him.

"Don't let them, Oliver," Timmons cried. "Don't *let* him—"

Laney pointed the gun in his right hand at Oliver. "Out of the way," he said.

Her last chance, they would guard him for the night and deliver him safe and sound in the morning. Mabel got up slowly, hand on the back of her chair. Only a boy, really, a skinny boy. No older, no bigger than Marie Eggena.

Timmons saw only the gun, and thought of Oliver's heart beats stopping or his brain smashed and gone. He tore himself from Laney's grasp just as Mabel leaped from behind, clawing, on Laney. The gun went off into the man who had flung himself protectively in front of Oliver's body.

The bullet went through his heart, exited at the back, and lodged itself in Oliver's lower ribcage. The two crashed backward onto the kitchen floor.

Laney extricated himself from Mabel, gave her a kick, leaped over the half-struggling pile of arms and legs and backs on the floor, ran out through the rain, listened for a moment at his van—no sirens—and then whisked on the other Laney and lifted down his motorcycle.

Lou never knew how and when Mabel made her exit. All she could hear was her own screaming, bending down in the kitchen, wrenching at Oliver's shoulders to pull him free of the ominously silent weight on top of him.

She found out later that Mabel Kovarski had walked down the long winding block to Farms River and thrown herself in. She was not a swimmer.

Lester Timmons had died instantly on the yellow-and-peach-patterned kitchen floor of 222 Lambert Road.

TWENTY-TWO

The killing—whether accidental or not—of one employee and the apparent suicide nearby of another employee on the same night put a decidedly different light on the proposed investigations at Bela-Goodwood.

("It all happened so fast that there's no way of telling whether he meant to shoot me—which I doubt—or Timmons, but he'd take care of that later, Timmons I mean, out of sight," Oliver told the police. "In a way poor Mabel killed Timmons, jumping on the kid from behind, except it would have been me if he hadn't . . ." The nurse said, "Don't distress the patient, please. That will be all for now.")

Telexes flew back and forth between Switzerland and New Jersey.

The story was given broad coverage in the Goodwood *Advocate* and the Farms River *News.* Much attention was paid to the unidentified robber-gunman who had falsely claimed to be with the Bela security force. A five-state hunt for him produced, eventually, nothing. The van had been abandoned beside the red house and was found to be registered in the name of a man who had been dead for several years.

A hysterical Lara, telephoned at her mother's the next morning by Ellen Parker, called Bela Security. From the Public Relations office, a smooth and capable young woman was dispatched by helicopter to Media, Pennsylvania. An accident, she explained, an attempted robbery or so it appeared, while Timmons had been visiting the house of a friend. It also appeared that he had died trying to save the life of the friend, who was blocking the robber's way out.

"In a way, Mrs. Timmons," said Public Relations, "a hero's death. You may not know that we have a special fund for acts of outstanding merit, at Bela." She handed her an envelope that held a certified check for ten thousand dollars. "This is just between you and me and our top management. We like to keep these matters confidential." Lara couldn't quite understand why, but she understood, through her tears, the check, "I suppose the reporters will be at me. No, I won't say anything about it." "And of course," went on Public Relations, "he was insured through our company plan for fifty thousand dollars. That, and beginning his pension payments, will be taken care of immediately."

"So you see," McCall said to Voss and Hoffer, after an early morning conference with Carrolton Deal, president of Bela-Goodwood, "instead of a little local dust-up, accident—who knows?—we'd be front page and TV news if the other thing got out. Can't you see the story? 'Does huge multinational Bela empire hide fifty would-be murderers within its walls?' "

Voss and Hoffer saw, their vision made even clearer by another telex from Bela Court, which ordered all investigations to be dropped immediately, to be resumed after a period of three months. Voss and Hoffer were to proceed to Dallas without delay and look into a disparity in the books of the assistant treasurer.

Before leaving on an afternoon plane, the two men were given a diplomatically luxurious lunch in the yellow private dining room. McCall was their host. The executive chef prepared a delectable wienerschnitzel for them, the wine steward chose a dry white vintage coincidentally labeled, Aurelio-Bela Cie.

Knowing McCall's tastes, the chef arranged for him what he called a millionaire's hamburger, finely chopped filet mignon, rare, with half an inch of thinly sliced Bermuda onions over it, in a freshly baked cheddar cheese bun. McCall liked to wash this down with Canadian ale served at 58 degrees.

Halfway through his veal, Voss said, "This Kalish."

McCall snapped to attention. "Yes, what about him?"

"Boys . . . well, as you people say, knock on any door, but . . ." He took a sip of his wine. "His name is in a half-dead file of ours. It's funny how you don't throw these bits and pieces away. A young man turned up at Bela Court last May, half-freaked, in tears, a mess. A friend of his, a Bert Orrin, was to meet him in Basle and never turned up. Do you recall, Hoffer?"

Hoffer, his mouth full of salad, shook his head.

"Well, anyway, we taped a blubbery kind of statement, that Orrin and Kalish had quarreled and that he knew for a fact that they had gone to make it up in Kalish's place on Fire Island, on the ocean . . . and that that was the last ever seen of Orrin. He was thought by the New York office to have disappeared for reasons of his own . . ."

Hoffer finished his meal and drained his wine glass. Sighing with satisfaction, he returned to the principal duty and pleasure of his life.

"When we resume our investigations here," he said "—and yes, now I remember the matter—let us say that Mr. Kalish might very well become, slightly rearranging the order of Timmons' list, Item Number One."

At a little after midnight the bullet was dug out from under Oliver's ribcage and he was pronounced officially out of danger, but informed that he would remain in his hospital bed for two days, to recuperate from surgery, shock and loss of blood.

On the second day, Veronica visited him, with flowers, fruit, and a book. "I don't know if you bring flowers to a man? But I did anyway. Isn't it awful? Poor Les." Her face shadowed. "But in a way he asked for it, didn't he. Though you know, in the last few months, up till it happened, I've never seen him so happy, he was a different man."

She was persuaded to eat some of the grapes and ripe apricots she had brought and Oliver produced the bottle he kept for Lou's visits; she had returned to New York that morning to finish out her working week.

"You can't imagine the uproar yesterday. And then there was an announcement on the p. a. saying Bela would close at three in memorial to the deaths of two valued employees."

She sipped her scotch. "I didn't tell you . . . Tuesday afternoon someone called me, and there was this horrible whispering, saying if Les had passed any information along to me I was to shut up about it or else. I don't know if it was a man or a woman. I was scared silly, you weren't there, so I went to Joe Wade, you know Joe? Mc'Call's assistant. I'd met him at a party a few weeks back and I thought he was sort of . . . sweet. I told him I didn't know what to do, I was frightened to go home to that empty apartment alone. And do you know what?"

From her general warm bloom, Oliver thought he knew what, but he politely asked the question.

"He followed my car home, and to protect me he stayed at my place all night." The wry, offhand Veronica suddenly blushed from hairline to white shirt collar. "Sitting *up*," she said.